"I hope you haven't made the *big* mistake of thinking he's going to marry you!"

In the appalled, deathly silence that followed these words, Dominic immediately leapt to his feet.

Swiftly bending down and scooping up something from the table, he quickly grabbed hold of Olivia's left hand.

"It's not the traditional diamond, of course." He grinned, slipping a tab from a soft drink can onto the third finger of her left hand. "However, as far as *I'm* concerned, I definitely intend to marry Olivia. So I think you can all regard this as our engagement party."

There was another moment's stunned silence, with everyone around the table staring openmouthed in astonishment as Dominic, pulling Olivia's trembling and dazed figure to her feet, placed his arms swiftly around her before claiming her lips in a long, warm and tender kiss.

Harlequin Presents® invites you to see how the other half marry in:

SOCIETY WEDDINGS

*They're gorgeous, they're glamorous...
and they're getting married!*

In this sensational five-book miniseries you'll be our VIP guest at some of the most-talked-about weddings of the decade—spectacular events where the cream of society gather to celebrate the marriages of dazzling brides and grooms in equally breathtaking international locations.

At each of these lavish ceremonies you'll meet some extraspecial men and women—all rich, royal or just renowned!—whose stories are guaranteed to capture your imagination, your heart...and the headlines! For in this sophisticated world of fame and fortune you can be sure of one thing: there'll be no end to scandal, surprises...and passion!

MARY LYONS

The Society Groom

SOCIETY WEDDINGS

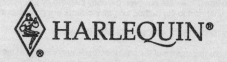

HARLEQUIN®

TORONTO • NEW YORK • LONDON
AMSTERDAM • PARIS • SYDNEY • HAMBURG
STOCKHOLM • ATHENS • TOKYO • MILAN • MADRID
PRAGUE • WARSAW • BUDAPEST • AUCKLAND

ISBN 0-373-12066-4

THE SOCIETY GROOM

First North American Publication 1999.

Visit us at www.romance.net

Printed in U.S.A.

CHAPTER ONE

IT WAS four o'clock on a freezing cold, dark winter's afternoon in the City of London as the large black limousine slowly came to a halt in front of the church.

'We're a bit early, aren't we?' Mark Ryland muttered, glancing nervously out of the vehicle at the long flight of steps leading up to the brilliantly lit church porch.

'Your bride-to-be gave me very clear instructions,' Dominic FitzCharles told him firmly. 'Not only was I to keep you as sober as possible at your stag party—but I was to make absolutely sure that we arrived at the church a good half-hour before the wedding.'

'Anyone would think I was still a kid,' Mark grumbled.

Dominic gave a quick shake of his dark head. 'Oh, no. You're merely that unimportant creature: the bridegroom!' he drawled with sardonic amusement. 'And as such—if you're a sensible man—you'll do *exactly* as you're told.'

'Thanks, pal!'

Dominic laughed. 'According to Sarah, she's already had to cope with *quite* enough problems. So, for you to be either suffering from a mammoth hangover or to be late for the ceremony would *definitely* be the last straw!'

'She's got a point,' Mark agreed as the uniformed chauffeur came around to open the passenger door.

Living in Hong Kong, where he was employed by a merchant bank, and only returning to Britain three days ago for his wedding, Mark had managed to avoid being dragged into any of the various traumas concerned with the organisation of his marriage to Sarah.

However, from what he could make out, it seemed that his fiancée and her mother had been at complete logger-heads with one another—barely able to agree about anything.

Fortunately, one of Sarah's friends had told her about Society Weddings—a business run by a girl her own age which specialised in taking charge of everything to do with such an occasion. In fact, the service offered by the firm seemed to cover every aspect of a wedding from the marriage ceremony and reception down to even finding the right shoes to match the bride's dress. And, in his fiancée's case, it had not only been able to take the burden from her shoulders, but also deal with her formidable mother, Mrs Turnbull.

'It's wonderful!' Sarah had breathed in relief down the phone, some months ago. 'Although I know Olivia's had plenty of experience in dealing with ultra-glamorous, so-phisticated events, she's been *so* down-to-earth and help-ful. And, what's more, she's managed to persuade Mummy to let me have *exactly* the sort of wedding that I've always wanted!'

So, thanks to the unknown Olivia, it had looked as if it was all going to be plain sailing as far as the arrange-ments for his forthcoming marriage were concerned.

But then his younger brother, James, had been suddenly rushed to hospital with acute appendicitis, only a few days ago. Which had left Mark in a dire fix, and urgently trying to find someone to act as his best man.

'Sarah and I are both so grateful,' Mark said as he stepped out of the limousine. 'Getting off the plane from Hong Kong to hear about poor old James was a bit of a shock. In fact, I honestly don't know *what* we'd have done if you hadn't come to our rescue.'

'Nonsense! It was the least I could do for an old school-friend.' Dominic grinned at the other man as he joined him on the pavement.

'Besides, it isn't the first time that I've acted as some-one's best man—and I don't suppose it will be the last,' he added, casting a critical eye over the groom's black morning tailcoat and pinstriped trousers—which, together with a crisp white shirt, doeskin waistcoat and pale grey tie, mirrored his own attire. 'Hold it just a second...' Dominic murmured, quickly reaching over to adjust the red carnation in the shorter man's buttonhole.

'OK—that's it. You're looking very smart!' he added, handing Mark a black silk top hat and gloves before giving the groom a cheerful, comforting slap on the back as they began mounting the long flight of steps leading up to the church. 'By the way, what's the latest news of your brother?'

'He seems to be recovering well from the operation. Although, as you can imagine, he's as sick as a parrot at being stuck in hospital and missing a good party,' Mark told him. 'All the same, I can't help wondering if maybe I *should* have cancelled the wedding and waited until he was back on his feet again, after all?'

'I don't suppose that Sarah's mother would have been too happy about the marriage being suddenly postponed at the last minute!' Dominic murmured blandly. Despite only having had one brief meeting with the hard faced, strongminded Mrs Turnbull, he was profoundly grateful that she wasn't going to be *his* mother-in-law!

'No, you're quite right—she wouldn't,' Mark agreed with a slight grimace, thanking his lucky stars that, following their honeymoon in the Caribbean, he and Sarah

would be living in Hong Kong for the next few years—
and well out of reach of her mother.

'And what about you? How come *you* haven't got married yet?' Mark asked, pausing halfway up the long, steep flight of steps. 'Isn't it about time you thought of settling down with one of your glamorous girlfriends?'

Dominic turned his dark head to gaze at him in astonishment. 'Good heavens! Why on earth would I want to get hitched?'

'I just thought...' Mark shrugged. 'I mean, there's all that business of needing a son to pass on the title, and...'

'You're way behind the times.' His friend gave a dry bark of laughter. 'Not only are the Government busy abolishing the House of Lords, but, quite frankly, no one cares very much about that sort of thing nowadays.'

'So there's been no pressure from your mother?' Mark queried, his voice heavy with disbelief as they continued on their way up the steps.

From what he recalled of their school days at Eton, the Dowager Countess of Tenterden was a frighteningly imperious lady: stiff with family pride and altogether a *very* tough act. So the chances of her *not* badgering Dominic to provide a son and heir to inherit his ancient title were very slim indeed!

'Ah! Well, yes...I must admit that my dear mama *has* expressed some firm views on the subject!' Dominic agreed ruefully, while nodding at some of his friends amongst the crowd of ushers waiting to greet the wedding guests and show them to their seats inside the church.

'However, I'm certainly in no hurry to "settle down", as you put it,' he continued. 'For one thing I'm far too busy nowadays. And for another...well, let's just say that I haven't yet found the right girl.'

Oh, yeah? Mark told himself with cynical amusement

as Dominic, his dark brows drawn together in a slight frown, took a quick step forward, peering into the dim interior of the large church porch.

He might have been living and working abroad for some time, but nevertheless Mark was perfectly well aware of Dominic's regular appearance in the newspaper gossip columns and glossy magazines. Not only was he a highly eligible bachelor, but his fast turnover of stunningly beautiful, glamorous girlfriends seemed guaranteed to keep him in the headlines for some time to come.

Which meant that if Dominic FitzCharles, fourteenth Earl of Tenterden, hadn't *yet* found the right girl…it certainly wasn't for lack of trying!

It was difficult for one man to judge another, of course. However, there was absolutely no doubt that, while Dominic might not be outstandingly handsome, women had always seemed to find his friend amazingly attractive.

With his thick, wavy dark hair, a slightly swarthy complexion, high cheekbones and Roman nose—together with a distinctly predatory glint in the heavy-lidded smokygrey eyes set beneath dark, quizzical eyebrows—Dominic had a disturbingly hawk-like, dangerous air about him. On top of which, since he was not only a peer of the realm but also extremely wealthy, *and* lived in a romantic old castle, it was no wonder that he appeared almost irresistible to the opposite sex!

Mark's slightly envious thoughts were interrupted as his friend, who'd left his side for a moment, returned with a puzzled frown in his face.

'That's odd,' Dominic murmured. 'I could have sworn… I thought I'd caught a glimpse of someone who seemed strangely familiar—although I can't recall where or when we might have met. But…' he shrugged his broad shoulders '...she now seems to have disappeared into thin air.'

'Oh, really? So after all your efforts to keep the groom as sober as a judge maybe it was the *best man* who drank too much last night?' Mark teased.

'You're probably right,' Dominic agreed with a slightly embarrassed, wry shrug of his shoulders as they entered the church and began walking slowly down the brightly lit nave towards their seats in the front pew, on the right-hand side of the aisle.

Unfortunately, Olivia Johnson was only too well aware of the identity of the tall, dark and attractive best man.

Earlier, while standing within the church porch, checking that the ushers had ample supplies of the Order of Service sheets, her eyes had slowly and inexorably been drawn towards the tall, broad-shouldered figure accompanying a shorter man as they'd mounted the church steps towards her.

I don't believe it! What on earth is *he* doing here? she'd asked herself incredulously, the blood draining from her face at the sight of the arrogant, hawk-like features of Dominic FitzCharles.

Feeling suddenly faint, as though she'd been hit by a violent blow to the solar plexus, Olivia had instinctively staggered back into a dark, shadowy far corner of the porch, desperately trying to pull herself together.

And then, as she'd heard the ushers outside on the steps calling out greetings to the two men, she'd realised that she'd just witnessed the arrival of the groom and his best man. Which had to mean that by some utterly disastrous, malign twist of fate it must be *Dominic* who'd been chosen to replace Mark Ryland's brother.

A moment later, suddenly overcome by panic as she'd

seen him moving determinedly through the crowd of ushers towards her, Olivia had taken to her heels. Quickly slipping through the half-open heavy oak door, she'd swiftly disappeared from sight inside the main body of the church.

Breathless and trembling with shock, her legs feeling as though they were made of cotton wool, Olivia had hurriedly made her way to a small side chapel, hidden from sight on the far side of the nave. Sinking weakly down onto a pew, and staring blindly at the flickering candles on the altar, she'd frantically tried to calm down and work out what she was going to do about this potentially disastrous situation.

Fortunately, it hadn't been very long before some small measure of common sense had come to her aid, and she'd gradually begun pulling herself together.

So…OK…it had been a shock, she told herself now firmly. But running away from a situation—however difficult-was obviously a very childish response, and certainly wasn't going to solve anything.

Although they now moved in quite different circles, and no longer had any friends in common, she really ought to have guessed that she was bound to meet Dominic again sooner or later. In fact, it had been downright stupid of her not to have already worked out what she was going to say, or do, if and when they bumped into one another. And why she hadn't prepared herself for just such an eventuality long before now, she had absolutely no idea.

Well, that wasn't strictly true, of course. Because no one with any sense would want to spend too much time thinking about unhappy episodes in their past. Not when they could hardly bear to recall the really awful, crippling shame of having once made such an almighty fool of themselves.

Besides, it must be at least ten years since that dreadfully embarrassing, quite horrendous episode involving herself and Dominic. Ten years in which Olivia knew that she'd changed beyond all recognition. Thankfully, she no longer bore any resemblance to that highly emotional eighteen-year-old, her head filled to the brim with romantic fantasies and madly in love with the wild, Byronic hero of her dreams.

Although, to be fair, she hadn't been the only silly, immature young girl overwhelmed by Dominic's devastating charm and overwhelming sex appeal. Or attracted, like a moth to a flame, by the highly glamorous, almost uncanny resemblance he bore to his ancestor—that famous seducer of beautiful women-King Charles II.

What an idiot she'd been! Olivia told herself, shaking her head at her own youthful folly. Anyone with even half an ounce of sense would have known that it would all end in tears. As indeed it had, she thought grimly, slowly rising to her feet and brushing the dust from her black velvet suit.

Taking a deep breath, she tried to clear her mind of the unhappy memories of the past. Quite apart from anything else, she couldn't afford to stay hidden away here, feeling sorry for herself. In fact, it was absolutely imperative that she got back to work as soon as possible.

As the owner and sole proprietor of Society Weddings—providing a service for those wishing to place the organisation of their wedding in safe, professional hands—Olivia knew that much of her success was the result of sheer hard work and careful planning. And she had quite enough to cope with in making sure that Sarah Turnbull's marriage proved to be the occasion of her dreams without having to worry about Dominic FitzCharles.

Of course, if she'd known that it was *he* whom Mark Ryland would choose as his best man when the groom's younger brother had been so unexpectedly taken ill with appendicitis, she might have been better prepared. But then, as she knew so well, life had a way of throwing rotten tomatoes in your way when you least expected it, and she was just going to have to cope with the situation as best she could.

Unfortunately, despite giving herself such really excellent advice, there seemed nothing Olivia could do to control the slightly sick feelings of nervous apprehension settling like a hard lump of concrete in her stomach.

Taking a deep breath, and fully determined to concentrate on her job, Olivia walked slowly out of the small side chapel into the main body of the church.

Please...*please* give Dominic FitzCharles a really *bad* case of amnesia! she prayed fervently, hoping against hope that a benevolent God would somehow save her from what she could only think of as a hideously embarrassing situation.

'I'm not sure that getting here so early was all that great an idea,' Mark said, shifting uncomfortably on the hard wooden pew and desperately wishing that he could get his hands on a stiff drink.

'It's just prewedding nerves,' Dominic drawled, smiling at the nervous, worried expression on the other man's pale face.

'It's all right for *you*!' Mark muttered grimly, ashamed to find himself feeling quite so tense. 'You may be in no hurry to get married, but I hope that I'm around to have a good laugh if and when some clever woman *does* manage to drag you to the altar.'

'Hey—relax!' Dominic murmured, gazing at his friend

with concern. 'Sarah's a wonderful girl, and I know that the two of you are going to be very happy. So just hang in there, OK?'

Mark nodded. 'Yeah...sorry about losing my cool like that. It's just...I don't know...' He gave a helpless shrug of his shoulders.

'It won't be long now,' Dominic told him comfortingly. 'By the way...' he added, attempting to distract his friend by turning his thoughts in another direction. 'Because of your brother's totally unexpected illness we haven't had time to discuss all the normal duties of a best man. So, what do you want me to do about paying the vicar? I've brought some money with me, just in case it might be necessary, and...'

'Oh, there's no need to worry,' Mark told him. 'Sarah's found this woman who's apparently taking care of all those boring, nitty-gritty details. In fact, as far as I can make out, she's handling just about everything.'

Dominic raised a dark, quizzical eyebrow. 'Everything?'

Mark nodded. 'According to Sarah, this woman has organised the whole bang-shoot. And, while it might be costing her father an arm and a leg, Sarah reckons it's worth every penny. If only for the fact that she's now having the sort of wedding *she* wants—and not something dreamed up by her mother.'

'That sounds like a damn good idea,' Dominic agreed as the sound of soft organ music and the increasing amount of noise and bustle indicated that the first guests were beginning to enter the church. 'Ah-ha...I *knew* I hadn't been mistaken!'

'Hmm...?'

Dominic nodded to the other side of the church, to where a girl was climbing up onto a pew, clearly with the aim of making a slight adjustment to a flower arrangement which had been placed on a high windowsill.

'That's the girl I saw earlier in the porch—when we first arrived. And I'm *still* quite certain that I've seen her somewhere before. But I can't recall exactly when or where...' he muttered, his dark brows drawn together in a distracted frown.

'Sorry—I haven't a clue who she is.' Mark gave a slight shrug. 'Although I must say,' he added, viewing the tight skirt of the girl's black velvet suit, momentarily riding up to reveal long, slim legs clothed in sheer black stockings, 'she's got a great pair of *very* sexy legs!'

'You're absolutely right,' Dominic drawled with amusement. 'But I don't think this is *exactly* the right moment to be saying so, do you? Not when you're supposed to be getting married in a few minutes' time!'

Mark grinned. However, before he could reply, his attention was claimed by the arrival of his parents, who were being shown to their seats in the pew directly behind him.

While Lady Ryland gave her son a quick kiss, and Lord Ryland shook his hand, gruffly wishing him 'the very best of luck, my boy', Dominic found himself becoming increasingly irritated at not being able to recollect precisely *where* he'd seen the tall, slim girl.

Moreover, if it didn't seem so utterly ridiculous, he might think that she was deliberately avoiding looking in his direction. In fact, despite not being able to catch more than a brief glimpse of a pale complexion and tawny-gold hair hidden beneath her wide-brimmed, black velvet hat, she still appeared disturbingly familiar—even while keeping her back firmly turned towards him.

With the arrival of Mrs Turnbull and the small bridesmaids, quickly followed by that of the bride and her father

at the church door, Olivia found herself far too busy to
spend any more time worrying about Dominic.

'You look absolutely wonderful!' she told Sarah with
a beaming smile, before quickly reassuring the other girl
that her groom had arrived, and everything was totally
under control. 'So just relax—and enjoy your wedding.'

'Yes, I know that I will…thanks to you!' Sarah said
with heartfelt gratitude as Olivia carefully adjusted the
cowl hood of the bride's long ivory velvet cloak, lined in
deep crimson satin, which flowed down to the ground and
behind her in a curved train.

'In fact, without your help, I'd be standing here dressed
like a fairy on the top of a Christmas tree!' Sarah added
with a ripple of laughter, and the two girls grinned at one
another as they recalled the many battles they'd had with
Mrs Turnbull.

'I want my daughter to look like a *proper* bride,' that
formidable lady had announced in a hard, no-nonsense
tone of voice on being first introduced to Olivia, some
months ago. 'Sarah might be marrying a lord's son—but
I'm not having any of his family thinking we don't know
what's what! Not when my husband's got more loose
change in his pocket than they've got in the whole of their
bank account,' she'd added grimly.

'You're absolutely right,' Olivia had murmured sooth-
ingly, well able to understand the older woman's determination not to be pushed around or over-awed by the
prospect of her daughter marrying into the aristocracy. In
fact, Mark's parents, Lord and Lady Ryland, were perfectly nice, ordinary people, distinctly nonsnobbish, and
very happy with their son's choice of bride.

It had, however, taken a great deal of time and trouble
on Olivia's part to convince Mrs Turnbull that the slim,

petite figure of her pretty darkhaired daughter would definitely *not* be seen to best advantage in the dress on which her mother had set her heart.

In fact, Olivia thought, it would have been downright cruel to force *anyone* to wear such a garment. With its heavily embroidered top, totally smothered in pearls and rhinestones, over a vast crinoline skirt composed of tier upon tier of heavy, brilliant white lace flounces, dotted with bows and posies of flowers—and yet more pearls and rhinestones—it had been a complete nightmare!

'I'll look dreadful—like some *huge* snowball!' Sarah had wailed in despair. 'Please help me, Olivia. You *must* try and make my mother see that I'm *far* too short to wear something like that. And that hard, bright white is absolutely the wrong colour for my skin.'

Eventually Olivia had managed to persuade Mrs Turnbull that 'less is more'—and to concentrate on elegance rather than magnificence. And the older woman had eventually agreed that maybe Sarah and Olivia's choice of wedding gown wasn't so bad, after all.

And now, as she gazed at the bride in her sophisticated, fluid sheath of pale ivory satin, a simple diamond hairband holding back her long black hair beneath the hood of her velvet cloak, Olivia realised that, despite the battles with Mrs Turnbull, it had all been worthwhile. Sarah looked not only stunningly beautiful, but also extremely elegant and thoroughly soignée.

'It was a great idea of yours to have the twins as my bridesmaids,' Sarah murmured, the battles she'd had with her mother all forgotten now as, wearing exactly the outfit she'd always wanted, she watched Olivia handing the tiny posies of red and pale cream roses to the two small girls.

'Don't they look adorable, Dad?' she asked her father as she smiled happily down at the dark-haired, five-year-old twin daughters of Mark's much older sister. Dressed in simple ivory velvet dresses, with wide crimson satin sashes tied at the back in a large bow, they looked enchanting.

'Aye, they do, lass,' Robert Turnbull agreed, nervously straightening his tie and wishing himself miles away.

Not that he didn't love his only daughter, he told himself firmly. But he was a plain-speaking Yorkshireman, and never happier than when running his large textile business. Although he got on right well with Mark's father, who seemed a sensible enough man, the sooner he could get back up North the happier he'd be.

'Hey—have you had a chance to get a good look at Mark's best man?' Sarah asked Olivia as the other girl bent down to straighten one of the little bridesmaid's ivory-coloured tights.

'Er...yes...' Olivia muttered, inwardly cursing the flush she could feel rising over her pale cheeks as she tried to concentrate on retying the bow of the little girl's red ballet shoes.

'Is he drop-dead gorgeous—or what?' Sarah giggled. 'At least half of the female guests invited to the wedding seem to be his old girlfriends, while the other half are intending to seriously chat him up at the reception!' she added with a grin, before nervously taking her father's arm as the organ began thumping out the first, loud chords of the 'Wedding March'.

Waiting until the bride and her retinue had begun walking slowly up the aisle, Olivia slipped into a seat at the back of the church.

But, despite the long length of the nave between them, she was still acutely aware of the broad-shouldered, dark figure of Dominic FitzCharles, standing beside the groom

as the vicar began the wedding service, joining Sarah and
Mark together in holy matrimony.

Despite the many other large, prestigious London hotels
which were often chosen for wedding receptions,
Claridge's Hotel was far and away Olivia's favourite
venue. Together with its wonderful Art Deco, nineteen-
thirties' style of decoration, the hotel's vast experience in
handling functions—from simple dinner parties to grand
balls attended by English royalty and the few remaining
crowned heads of Europe—meant that she could safely
leave all arrangements in the capable hands of the hotel's
staff.

And she'd been quite right. It was now an hour since
the bride and groom had arrived at the hotel following
their marriage, and everything seemed to be going with a
swing.

The large reception room looked magnificent. The crys-
tal chandeliers were casting a sparkling glow over the
smartly dressed guests; the many huge flower arrangements filled the air with a delicious perfume; and an army
of waiters were making sure that the champagne was flowing like water. All perfect ingredients for a great party!

However, as she now stood in a far corner of the large
reception room, quickly glancing down at her watch as
the happy couple circulated amongst their guests, Olivia
knew that there were still some hours to go before she
could relax.

With the groom only returning to Britain just a few
days before his marriage, it hadn't been the easiest of
weddings to arrange. Especially as Sarah had had some
firm ideas about the reception.

'I want to have some sort of dinner-dance,' she'd said,
before adding with a frown, 'But what do we do with the

all those elderly relatives and friends of my parents? They're going to simply hate the idea of dancing, since most of them will just want to sit around, catching up on the family gossip.'

However, after carefully going through the proposed list of guests, and noting that many of Sarah and Mark's friends worked in the City of London, Olivia had put forward a suggestion that the wedding should take place in one of the ancient City churches on a late Friday afternoon.

'I know it's slightly unusual,' she'd told Mrs Turnbull and her daughter. 'But it will make it a lot easier for busy men and women to attend the wedding at the end of a working week before going on to a reception in a hotel such as Claridge's. And if you start with a champagne reception—including the usual speeches and cutting the wedding cake—those who wish to do so can then leave, with the younger guests staying on to enjoy a buffet dinner and dance.'

'That's a brilliant idea!' Sarah had exclaimed. And even Mrs Turnbull had grudgingly agreed that it did seem to cater for just about all their guests.

However, now, despite being busily engaged in making sure that the reception was proceeding smoothly, Olivia was only too well aware that she still had a major problem on her hands.

Right from the moment he'd arrived at the hotel with the bride and groom, she'd been acutely aware that Dominic FitzCharles—clearly unused to being thwarted in any way—was still determined to find an answer to the puzzle which had been troubling him since his arrival at the church.

The damn man's as stubborn as a mule, Olivia had told herself grimly, doing her best to ignore the granite-hard, clear grey eyes regarding her intently as she'd moved about the room, making sure that the influx of guests were being properly looked after. Luckily, Dominic had been forced to stand in the receiving line, together with Sarah and Mark and their parents—so she'd been quite safe for a while.

However, after all the guests had arrived, and Dominic had at last been able to leave the receiving line, Olivia had found herself beginning to panic. Maybe she was just being paranoid, but it had seemed that he was deliberately 'stalking' her through the crowded throng of guests, smoothly greeting his friends and acquaintances while all the time firmly keeping her tall, slim figure in view.

He'd almost caught up with her as she'd been checking over the timing of the speeches with the Toastmaster, hired for the occasion. Luckily, she'd managed to quickly make her escape by hurriedly taking refuge in the ladies' powder room.

Suddenly feeling exhausted by the stress and strain engendered by Dominic's totally unexpected appearance as Mark Ryland's best man, she'd sunk down onto a padded stool, removing her wide-brimmed black hat and gazing helplessly at herself in the mirror.

'Come on! For heaven's sake, pull yourself together— and get a grip on the situation!' she'd muttered grimly under her breath, grimacing at the sight of her pale cheeks and the tense, strained lines around the wide green eyes staring back at her, cloudy with fear and apprehension.

While she couldn't, of course, have stayed hidden in the powder room for very long, it had at least given her the opportunity to do something about her hair. And, there was no doubt, after vigorously brushing her long hair before once again winding it into a neat coil at the back of her head, that she had felt a whole lot better.

Leaving her large hat in the care of the cloakroom lady, and confident that she was once again maintaining her normal 'strictly business' appearance, she'd cautiously made her way back to the reception.

Now, following her signal, the Toastmaster gathered together the chief members of the wedding party at the far end of the room, before calling for silence to enable an elderly relative of the bride to propose the health of the happy couple.

So used to wedding speeches—which could occasionally go on for an inordinate length of time!—Olivia wasn't really listening to what was being said at the far end of the room. Until, to her complete astonishment, she caught the sound of her own name.

Quickly jerking to attention, she gazed over the heads of the crowd towards where, most unusually, she saw that the bride had seized hold of the microphone.

'...and we're so happy to see you all here today.' Sarah gave the guests a broad grin. 'I've already thanked my parents, and everyone else connected with our marriage, but I do want everyone to know that without the help of Olivia Johnson and her firm Society Weddings, which took all the strain out of what could have been a tense time before our wedding, Mark and I might well have run off on our own and eloped to Gretna Green!'

Oh, Lord! It looks as if Sarah has *really* hit the champagne bottle, more than somewhat! was the first thought to enter Olivia's head, as a ripple of laughter and applause rang around the room.

And then, as she saw Dominic give a quick snap of his fingers—the gesture accompanied by an expression of triumph and satisfaction flickering briefly across his handsome face—Olivia realised that any hope of her remaining anonymous as far as Dominic was concerned was now a

MARY LYONS

complete waste of time. A fact emphasised as, in his role of best man, he stepped forward to make the final speech of the day, before once more proposing the health of the bride and groom.

It was an accomplished, smooth performance. Although Olivia could have done without the heavily cynical, distinct emphasis in his voice when welcoming so many *'old friends'* to the wedding.

However, it looked as though the rotten man must be able to move with the speed of light. Because, only a moment or two after the bride and groom had cut the cake, Olivia suddenly became aware that the tall, broad-shouldered figure of Dominic FitzCharles was now standing by her side.

'Well, well, how very nice to see you again, Olivia. And after all these years!' he drawled coolly, smiling sardonically down at the pale-faced, slim figure of the girl who'd been so clearly avoiding him for some hours.

CHAPTER TWO

'IT'S been a long time since we last saw one another,' Dominic drawled smoothly.

'Yes, it has,' Olivia agreed, thoroughly rattled by his sudden, unexpectedly swift appearance at her side.

'So…what have you been doing with yourself all these years?'

She shrugged. 'Not a lot.'

'Oh, really?' he murmured. 'You certainly seem to have been quite busy today.'

'Well, yes. As you can see, I run a business arranging weddings,' she muttered, avoiding his eyes as she gazed past him at the crowded throng of guests.

He gave a short bark of dry laughter. 'Yes—I *had* rather gathered that fact,' he told her, not bothering to hide the note of hard irony in his deep voice. 'Is it a successful business?'

She gave another shrug of her slim shoulders. 'I make a reasonable living!'

'I'm glad to hear it,' he drawled, his lips twitching with wry amusement and clearly not at all perturbed by the girl's obvious reluctance to continue the conversation. 'But what about your private life?'

'What about it?' she queried stonily, still avoiding his gaze as her eyes flicked nervously around the room, frantically searching for some avenue of escape from the tall, dark figure now standing so close to her.

'Well, now…' he drawled mockingly. 'I was merely wondering if you are happy and content with your life?

Whether you're married or single? Are you still living in the country—or do you have a home here in London? Nothing very dramatic,' he added with a grin. 'Just the normal, boring type of questions that one usually asks at this kind of function.'

'Yes, I am happy. No, I'm not married—and, yes, I live in London,' she snapped tersely. 'And now, if you don't mind, I really think that I must go and...'

'Oh, but I *do* mind,' he murmured, quickly taking hold of her arm and leading her reluctant, nervously protesting figure to a small alcove in the far corner of the room.

'No...really...I've still got a lot of work to do, and...'

'It can wait,' he said, firmly sitting her down on a small padded bench, effectively screened from the rest of the room by heavy velvet curtains.

'We've both been on duty quite long enough. So I feel we're entitled to a short break, don't you?' Dominic continued, not waiting for an answer as he added, 'I'm just going to get us both a drink. But don't make the mistake of trying to escape me yet again, hmm?'

Despite the cool smile on his face, there was no mistaking the intimidating, icy note of menace in his voice as he stood staring down at her for a moment, before swiftly turning on his heels and striding across the room in search of a waiter.

As she watched Dominic's tall, commanding figure smoothly making his way through the crowd, Olivia desperately tried to bring her chaotic thoughts and emotions under some sort of control. To have so unexpectedly met again the man who'd once meant so much to her, and from whom she had parted so abruptly and painfully, was proving to be almost more than she could cope with.

It was ridiculous to be meekly sitting here—doing as she was told and not daring to move, just as though she was a naughty child, she told herself, suddenly irritated with herself for being so weak and feeble. However, as she acknowledged with a heavy sigh, it was obviously pointless to continue trying to evade any contact with Dominic. There were still some hours to go before the end of the wedding reception—and she could hardly keep ricocheting back and forth around this large room, attempting to avoid the man. She would just end up looking totally ridiculous.

In any case, she was damned if she was prepared to let Dominic guess just how devastated she'd been by the abrupt termination of their brief love affair. In fact, if she'd had any sense at all—and hadn't been so thrown by his sudden appearance by her side a few moments ago— she ought to have lied her head off and told him that she was happily married. Or at least laid claim to a highly active sex life with a whole string of highly glamorous lovers.

Come on...*come on*! You've got to get a grip on yourself. You're not a teenager any more, she told herself roughly. You're a successful businesswoman of twenty-eight years of age. So there's absolutely no reason why you should put up with any nonsense, she was telling herself firmly as she saw Dominic returning back across the room, a glass of champagne in each hand.

He hasn't changed at all, she thought, her mood swinging from firm resolution to nervous misery in the twinkling of an eye; she instantly recognised an old, all too familiar ache in her body at the sight of the most devastatingly attractive man she'd ever known.

There were, of course, a few threads of silver amidst the dark hair at his temples, and his face was now somewhat leaner, with a more stern expression than she remembered. There also appeared to be a more forceful, autocratic stance to his figure. However, that was perhaps not so surprising, since Dominic had inherited both his title, the huge castle in Kent and the management of ten thousand acres on the death of his father some years ago. And with such an inheritance had also come *noblesse oblige*: the heavy duties and responsibilities of those born to wealth and grandeur.

While she might not have physically laid eyes on him for the past ten years, Olivia was well aware—from both the newspaper columns and glossy magazines—that if Dominic played hard, he also worked very hard as well. He sat on the boards of various large companies involved in farming, he'd been appointed by the Queen as Deputy Lord Lieutenant for the County of Kent, and, as she knew from her own father, who lived nearby, Dominic was also president of many various local charities.

However, as he now handed her a glass of champagne, she realised that while his outward appearance might have changed slightly over the past ten years, he still possessed that glittering aura which instinctively drew people to him: an almost sinister air of stillness and self-control that had always set him apart from anyone else she'd ever known.

'We've a lot of news to catch up on,' he said, sitting down beside her on the small bench. 'How is Lord Bibury these days? I haven't seen him for some years.'

'Oh, Dad's all right,' she muttered, trying to inch away from the tall, broad-shouldered figure, whose hard, muscular thigh was now pressed closely to her own. 'Actually...actually, my father *isn't* too good these days,' she added, her attention slightly distracted as she realised that it was a waste of time to try avoiding contact with Dominic—since the bench had clearly been designed for midgets!

'I'm sorry to hear that,' he murmured, his lips twitching with wry amusement at the girl's obvious reluctance to sit too close to him. 'What's the problem?'

Olivia sighed. 'Poor old Dad got totally hammered in the Lloyds of London debacle.'

'What bad luck.' Dominic frowned. 'Did he lose a lot of money?'

'Just about everything.' She sighed heavily. 'We've managed to hang onto the house. But I'm afraid all the land was sold some time ago.'

'And what about your stepmother?' he queried. 'I can't imagine Pamela having been too happy about that sort of situation?'

'No, she wasn't!' Olivia agreed with a snort of grim laughter as she stared down at the glass of champagne in her hand.

A whip-thin, socially ambitious blonde woman, who'd managed to sink her hooks into Olivia's father only a year after his wife's death, Pamela had been responsible for making Olivia's teenage life an absolute misery. So when Pamela—the archetypal wicked stepmother—had been faced with the sudden collapse of her comfortable life, and her role as Lady of the Manor, Olivia hadn't been in the least surprised by her subsequent actions.

'When the going gets tough—the tough get going. *Literally*, in the case of my stepmother!' Olivia told him with another bark of harsh laughter. 'Because she quickly dumped my father and is now married to a rich northern industrialist—Reg Plumley. Although, as you might guess, she still calls herself "Lady" Plumley—if and when she thinks she can get away with it!'

Dominic gave a low, soft rumble of laughter. 'She really was a dreadful woman, wasn't she?'

'Oh—absolutely *awful*!' Olivia agreed, the past ten

years seeming to fade away as she grinned up at him, their mutual sense of humour and appreciation of the ridiculous aspects of life clearly as strong as it had always been.

'It's good to see that you haven't *really* changed at all,' he murmured, placing an arm around her slim figure and pulling her closer to his strong, firm body. 'I've missed you all these years.'

It didn't need the warm, sensual note in his deep voice, or the decided glint in those gleaming grey eyes beneath their heavy lids, to set the alarm bells ringing loudly in her brain. At the first touch of his strong arm about her shoulders Olivia had immediately begun to feel almost sick and breathless. And, with her face now only inches away from his own, every nerve-end in her body seemed to be tingling in response to this man's extremely dangerous, rampant sex appeal.

Desperately trying to combat the insidious aura of sensuality which had always seemed to surround Dominic— and was still as highly potent today as it had been ten years ago—Olivia made a determined effort to pull herself together.

'You're quite wrong,' she told him as firmly as she could, although she was well aware of the slightly tremulous wobble in her voice as she quickly jumped to her feet. 'I *have* changed. In fact, I'm now an *entirely* different person—and light years away from the silly, immature girl that you once knew. Believe me, she was dead and buried a long time ago,' Olivia added with a grim smile.

'As for that ridiculous statement about your having missed me—I've never heard such nonsense!' she continued, calmly handing him her still full glass of champagne. 'I've got eyes in my head, and I can read the newspapers and gossip columns along with everyone else. So, quite frankly, Dominic—' she gave a short bark of sardonic laughter '—I suggest that you save that sort of chat-up line for some other young girl who hasn't yet cut her wisdom teeth!

'And now, if you'll excuse me...' She quickly straightened her velvet jacket, before brushing some fluff from her skirt. 'I must go and see how the arrangements for the buffet supper are coming along.'

How she was able to walk away from him with her head held high and with such firm, determined steps, Olivia never quite knew. However, the knowledge that she'd *at last* had the great pleasure and satisfaction of being able to give Dominic such a well-deserved put-down was definitely a soothing balm for her strained emotions.

She might well regret having been so foolish in the past. But at least she'd now drawn a line under that silly, immature affair which had taken place between them so long ago. Because there was no way a proud, arrogant man like Dominic FitzCharles would ever again try to smooth talk his way into her affections.

However, if Olivia had paused to look over her shoulder, she might well have been surprised to see that far from being dejected and cast down—or, indeed, furiously angry at being given the cold shoulder by an old girlfriend—Dominic was regarding her progress across the floor with a raised, dark quizzical eyebrow and a highly amused smile on his lips.

'Well, well! Now, that really is *very* interesting,' he murmured softly to himself as he rose to his feet, handing the two glasses of champagne to a passing waiter. It definitely seemed as if the once soft, shy young girl had now developed some very sharp claws!

Moreover, he was intrigued to note over the next few

hours that Olivia had indeed changed over the past ten years. In fact, it was obvious that a considerable number of men, both married and single, were attracted to the tall and slim tawny-haired girl as she moved confidently and serenely through the crowd of guests, making sure that no one had an empty glass and that all the arrangements went smoothly. Yes…it certainly looked as though the pretty young cygnet had now become an extremely graceful, elegant swan.

As far as Olivia was concerned, while she was doing her best to appear cool, calm and collected, she was actually in a state of utter panic. *Where on earth were the bride and groom?*

All thought of Dominic had been driven completely from her mind as she hunted high and low for the happy couple. Goodness knows where they'd got to. But since they were due, in five minutes' time, to open the dinner-dance by taking the floor in a slow waltz, it was imperative that she track them down as soon as possible.

'Oh—*thank heavens!* I thought you really *had* taken off for Gretna Green!' she exclaimed, beaming with relief as she spotted Mark and Sarah coming out of a lift on the ground floor. 'Where on earth have you been?'

A flush rose up over Mark's face as he adjusted his tie and pulled down his waistcoat. 'Well, the thing is…'

'The thing is,' Sarah echoed, her eyes gleaming with laughter, 'Mark and I decided to nip upstairs to our fantastically luxurious, glamorous bridal suite—to see if the bed was *really* quite as comfortable as it looked!'

'Oh, honestly!' Olivia muttered, unable to repress a grin as she quickly straightened the bride's dress, adjusting the diamond headband before brushing out the tangles in Sarah's long black hair. 'There's a time and place for everything, you know!'

'That's what we thought, too,' Sarah agreed solemnly, before almost collapsing in a fit of giggles.

'I'm glad that you've had a good time.' Olivia grinned. 'However, can you both get yourselves onto the dance floor as soon as possible? Because to tell the truth, Mark, your new mother-in-law looks as if she's going to blow a gasket any minute!'

'Oh, Lord! Thanks for the warning,' Mark muttered, quickly grabbing hold of Sarah's hand and hurrying towards the ballroom.

'There was nothing to worry about,' she assured Mrs Turnbull, who'd clearly been getting up a full head of steam about the temporary disappearance of her daughter. 'Sarah just needed to make a minor repair to her dress,' Olivia lied smoothly, well used to coping with new brides and grooms unable to resist an early celebration of their marriage.

Luckily, the remainder of the evening passed without another hitch. Although, as very much a spectator at these sort of events, Olivia was unable to avoid the sight of Dominic, constantly surrounded by a large number of highly attractive women.

And good luck to him! she told herself firmly. She simply wasn't interested in him one way or another. Although, if she was going to be strictly honest with herself, she *really* hadn't cared for the sight of that young blonde starlet—regularly featured in some of the more downmarket, glossy magazines—who'd been all over Dominic like a rash while they'd enjoyed a smoochy dance, late in the evening.

And then, soon after midnight, the bride and groom were being waved off to their bridal suite. Although it was another hour before most of the young guests decided to call it a day, leaving the very tired but happy parents of the bride and groom to also seek their beds.

Well—that's another job well done, Olivia told herself as she shepherded the last stragglers to the door, leaving them in the capable hands of the uniformed doorman in his top hat, either to order taxis or see them to their own vehicles.

Collecting her own hat from the ladies' cloakroom, and thanking the manager on duty for all the help and expertise of his staff, she at last felt able to make her own way home.

Unfortunately, although there was normally no problem in finding a taxi in Brook Street, the mass exodus of guests had obviously depleted the usual number of vehicles normally to be found outside the hotel. Standing outside on the street, stamping her feet to keep warm, Olivia found herself regretting that she hadn't, in fact, realised that there might be a problem and sensibly parked her own car around the corner earlier in the day.

'It's funny how there never seems to be a taxi when you want one, isn't it, miss?' the doorman said with a grin, stepping out into the street and looking up and down the road. 'However, I'm sure there'll be a taxi along in a minute.'

'I hope so,' she muttered, pulling her jacket tightly about her cold figure. 'At least it isn't raining,' she added, her teeth chattering as a blast of icy wind swept down the street.

'You waiting for a taxi, lady?'

'Yes, I am...' she muttered, her eyes widening as she looked up to see a large blue Range Rover drawn up before her shivering figure.

'You'd better hurry up and jump in.' Dominic grinned

at her through the open driver's window. 'Unless, of course, you don't mind freezing to death out there!'

'Well...' Olivia glanced up and down the deserted street, but there was clearly no sight of a taxi. 'Oh, all right,' she agreed with a helpless shrug as she went around to the passenger door. 'But you don't know where I live. It might not be on your way home.'

'I expect I'll manage to find the way—to wherever it is.' Dominic grinned again. Then, as she still hesitated, he told her roughly not to be such a fool. 'You could be waiting out here for ages,' he pointed out. 'Still, if you don't mind catching pneumonia that's your problem, not mine!'

'Thanks!' she grumbled, before quickly deciding that he was quite right. There was no sight of any other form of transport, and the thought of having to stand outside the hotel, freezing to death in this weather, was more than she could face.

'I live in Holland Park,' she said, hitching up her skirt and climbing up into the high vehicle. 'I hope that's not too much out of your way? Are you planning to drive back down to Kent tonight?' she asked breathlessly, not at all sure that it was sensible to accept a lift from Dominic, but not seeing that she had any alternative.

'No, I've got a small pad in Chelsea which I and my sisters use when we have to stay overnight in London,' he told her, putting the car in gear and driving off down the street.

With very little traffic around at that time of night, it should have been a quick and easy journey home. But as he drove them up Park Lane and around Marble Arch, towards the Bayswater Road, she began to find the atmosphere within the large vehicle becoming increasingly claustrophobic.

There was absolutely no reason for her to be feeling quite so tense and apprehensive—not to say distinctly nervous. Nevertheless, she was finding it difficult to combat the strangely insidious, intimate atmosphere within the close confines of the vehicle. Even after tearing her gaze away from the sight of his strong hands gripping the wheel, and closing her eyes as she leaned back against the headrest, all her senses appeared to be disturbingly alive, acutely conscious of the scent of his cologne, and the slight movements of the tall, powerful body seated so closely to her own.

'I think you'd better direct me from here on,' Dominic said quietly as they sped through Notting Hill Gate and entered Holland Park Avenue.

However, just as she was telling him to take the next left turning into Holland Park, she was surprised to find their way barred by bollards with flashing lights and two police vehicles parked across the entrance of the mews.

'What the heck...?' she muttered as a policeman approached and Dominic pressed a button to lower his window.

'Sorry, sir—we've got a slight problem here,' the man told him. 'It seems that there's a burst water main, and—'

'Oh—not *again*!' Olivia groaned.

'Yes, I'm afraid so, miss.' The policeman shrugged. 'Someone from the Fire Brigade told me that there's often a problem here in Holland Park Avenue. Although I understand the mains are due to be replaced in the near future.'

'That'll be the day,' she grumbled, fed up to the back teeth with the aged water pipes which had caused so much trouble for such a long time.

'How long will it take before it's mended?' Dominic enquired.

The other man shrugged. 'I'm told there's no access to either end of the mews for the next four hours at least. And I shouldn't be at all surprised if it doesn't take a lot longer than that,' he added gloomily.

'OK. Thanks,' Dominic said, closing the window and quickly putting the car into reverse before speeding off back down Holland Park Avenue.

'What are you doing? Where do you think you're going?' she cried, feeling stunned by the speed of events, and desperately trying to work out where she was going to spend the night.

'I've got a spare bedroom, so it makes sense for you to stay the night in my house,' he told her. 'Unless, of course, you'd prefer that I take you to a hotel?'

Olivia turned to glare at him in the darkness. 'Oh, yes— that's a *great* idea!' she grumbled sarcastically. 'First of all I've got to find a hotel that's still open at this time of night. And even if I do they probably wouldn't be willing to take me in—not without any luggage, or even a toothbrush to my name,' she added grimly.

Dominic merely shrugged his shoulders. 'It's up to you, of course. Although it doesn't look as if you've got much choice, does it?'

'No.' She gave a heavy sigh. 'You're quite right—it doesn't.'

However, by the time he was parking the large Range Rover in Markham Square, Olivia had managed to overcome her instinctive anger and annoyance at finding herself at the mercy of some arbitrary fate.

'I'm sorry,' she said. 'I really ought to apologise for being so ratty just now. I expect that I'm just a bit tired— and I was looking forward to returning home and putting my feet up. But I shouldn't have taken it out on you,' she added, turning to give him a brief, apologetic smile. 'And I really am very grateful for the offer of a bed tonight.'

'There's no need to apologise.' He waved a hand dismissively in the air. 'We've both had a long, tiring day.'

'Just a minute,' she said as he released his seatbelt and opened his door to alight from the vehicle. 'This "spare room" of yours? I take it it really *does* exist—and isn't some figment of your imagination?'

Dominic gave a low rumble of sardonic laughter. 'Relax! I have at least *three* spare bedrooms—so you'll be able to take your pick,' he told her, before coming round to open the passenger door. 'Although, of course, I'd be *more* than happy to offer you the use of my own bedroom.'

'If it includes you as well—the answer is thanks, but no thanks!' she snapped, her nerves not improved by the sight of his wide grin and the glint of ironic amusement in his eyes, clearly visible beneath the sodium glare of a nearby streetlight.

'Calm down, darling,' he drawled, helping her down from the vehicle and issuing her in through the front door of a large house. 'I can promise you, on my word of honour, that I won't lay a hand on you.'

'You'd better keep your promise—or you'll be sorry!' she muttered grimly as he led the way into a sitting room.

So much for the 'small pad in Chelsea'! Olivia told herself, recalling how Dominic had described his home in London as she gazed around the large, elegantly decorated room. Having been forced to save up every penny for her own small mews house, she was in no doubt that this huge building would, on the open market, fetch well over a million pounds.

'Now...why don't we both relax and have a drink?' he was saying, with a slow, sensual smile which practically made her hair stand on end. 'I can offer you some whisky, or brandy, or...'

Olivia gave a nervous shake of her head. 'No, thanks all the same, but I'm really feeling very tired. It's been a long day,' she added quickly. 'If...if you don't mind, I'd like to go to my room straight away.'

'Of course,' he said, opening the door and waving for her to go ahead of him up the wide flight of stairs, before leading her along the landing and throwing open the door of a large guest room.

'As you see,' Dominic told her, walking across the large room and opening a door in the far corner, 'this guest bedroom has its own *en suite* bathroom. I'll just check...' He switched on the lights and peered around the door. 'Yes, there appear to be plenty of towels. But let me know if there's anything else you require, OK?' he murmured as he retraced his steps across the room, giving her a slight smile before closing the bedroom door behind him.

Well, things could definitely be a lot worse, Olivia told herself some time later, almost groaning with pleasure as she lay back in the deliciously oily, highly perfumed bath water, closing her eyes and letting all the stresses and strains of the day drain out of her tired body.

Although she'd been fed up at not being able to relax in her own bed, it was kind of Dominic to have placed a spare room at her disposal. Not that he wasn't the same tricky, conniving, two-timing rat that she'd known all those years ago, of course, she quickly reminded herself. Leopards didn't change their spots—right? And the way that blonde bimbo had practically *glued* herself to his tall, broad-shouldered figure on the dance floor had been nothing short of disgraceful!

But why should she care? It was, after all, years since

she'd first tumbled headlong into love with Dominic. But she was no longer a silly teenager, and if he wanted to make an exhibition of himself—or go to bed with half the women in London, for that matter—it was absolutely nothing to do with her.

Well, yes...OK...she *had* been upset to see him again. But that was only because his appearance at the wedding had been so totally unexpected. Any woman would be likely to feel slightly shocked and thrown a bit off base by the sudden appearance of an old flame. So her reaction had been a quite normal one, she assured herself firmly. And, after a good night's sleep, she would be perfectly capable of saying a cheerful goodbye to her host before going back to her own home and never giving him another thought.

Having sorted out the current situation to her own satisfaction, Olivia felt a whole lot more cheerful. Of course, the relaxing effect of a hot bath had a lot to do with it, she told herself, climbing out of the deep tub and wrapping a thick fluffy towel about her slim figure. However, it wasn't until she was walking slowly back into the bedroom that she suddenly realised she had a slight problem.

Although many of her friends slept in the nude, she'd never been at all keen on getting into a cold bed stark naked. And, since she'd made the mistake of rinsing out her underwear and leaving it to dripdry by morning, she was now well and truly stuck without anything to wear. However, just as she was wondering whether to wrap a fresh, clean towel about herself, in place of her usual night attire, she heard a brisk tap on her door.

'I hope you haven't gone to sleep in the bath,' Dominic's amused voice called out from the other side of the door. 'Would you care for the use of a spare dressing gown?'

Hesitating for a moment, she quickly wrapped the towel more tightly about her before opening the door.

'Yes, I would,' she admitted, noting from his damp, curly dark hair that he, too, must have recently had a bath or shower. And, instead of his elegant morning dress, Dominic was now wearing a knee-length, dark red silk dressing gown. And not much else, if the sight of his long, tanned bare legs was anything to go by, she told herself grimly as he walked across the room to open the door of a large cupboard.

'There's a spare gown in here,' he said, taking out a long, silky garment and handing it to her. 'There are also one or two nighties—but I'll leave you to make your own choice.'

'That's very kind of you, but I really don't think that—'

'Don't worry—they are definitely *not* my old girlfriends' castoffs!' He turned to give her a quick grin as he closed the door of the wardrobe. 'My older sister, Connie, was over from the United States last year, and she left some articles of clothing behind when she returned home.'

'Oh, right,' Olivia muttered, feeling slightly flustered by his uncanny ability to read her mind. Because of course she couldn't have faced wearing anything left behind by any of his usual girlfriends. Most of whom—if the glossy magazines were to be believed—consisted of glamorous film stars with truly *amazing* chest measurements.

'Is there anything else I can do for you?' he asked, moving slowly towards her.

'No, I'm fine,' she murmured, instinctively backing away from his advancing figure.

There *really* ought to be some sort of law to prevent highly attractive, sexy men from walking around practically stark naked, she told herself grimly. Because the

sight of his tall figure in the deep red dressing gown—
despite the fact that it was tightly belted about his slim
waist—was enough to make any poor, susceptible woman
feel distinctly lightheaded.

Viewing the soft, silky material clinging so closely to
his damp body, emphasising his broad shoulders, slim
hips and strong, muscular chest covered in dark curly hair,
Olivia could almost physically feel her senses being assailed by his overpowering aura of sheer, rampant mas-
culinity.

'I think that I've got everything,' she muttered helplessly, moistening her lips, which had suddenly become
dry and parched. 'I expect...I'm sure...that you must be
as tired as I am...' Her voice trailed away as she noticed
his eyes gleaming with amusement at her obvious confusion.

'Are you *quite* sure that you've got everything you
want...?' he drawled softly, the low, sensual note in his
voice playing havoc with her nervous system, her pulse
almost racing out of control as she took another step backwards.

But then, as she felt her spine jar against the wall beside
the door, she made a desperate effort to pull herself together.

'I—I'm not interested in playing stupid games,' she
told him as firmly as she could, bitterly aware of the
breathless, hoarse note in her voice as she clutched the
towel tightly about her slim figure. 'So, will you *please*
leave this room—and return to your own bedroom.'

'Of course I will,' he murmured, continuing to move
forward until his figure was virtually touching her own.
'I was merely intending to kiss you goodnight before I
go.'

'Cut it out—Dominic!' she protested huskily as she felt

the weight of his hard, firm body pressing her up against the wall. 'I thought you'd promised not to lay a hand on me?'

'You're absolutely right!' he agreed with a low rumble of laughter, before placing the palms of his hands flat on the wall either side of her head. 'And I have every intention of keeping my promise,' he murmured, leaning forward to brush his mouth across her quivering lips with a teasing, erotic sensuality that left her breathless with desire.

'Goodnight, Olivia,' he breathed softly against her mouth as his kiss deepened, his lips and tongue seducing her into a state of helpless, trembling rapture. And then, quite suddenly, he raised his dark head and she found herself released from the heavy pressure of his hard body.

For a brief, fleeting moment, it seemed as though the gleaming grey eyes held a strange message as he stared intently down at her, an oddly tense, strained expression on his handsome tanned face. But by the time she'd managed to pull her dazed mind and body together Olivia realised she must have been mistaken. Because he appeared to be regarding her with a perfectly normal, light smile on his lips.

'I'll see you in the morning,' he murmured, running a finger gently down over her soft cheek before swiftly leaving the room.

...dismissive effect she was having on her long dormant emotions, who clearly lay at the root of her problem.

Eventually, giving up the unequal struggle, she threw back the sheet and blanket and slipped out of bed. Padding on the warm floor, she made her way across the carpet towards a large window on the far side of the room.

...

CHAPTER THREE

DESPITE being tired, and weary from having been on her feet all day, Olivia found herself tossing and turning as she stared wide-eyed up at the ceiling of the guest room in Dominic's house.

There seemed no immediate, obvious reason why she was finding it so difficult to go to sleep. Not only was it a very comfortable bed, but she'd also enjoyed the luxurious comfort of a hot bath: two of the items normally recommended for those seeking oblivion in sleep.

Sighing heavily, Olivia realised that there was no point in trying to fool herself any longer. Because that goodnight kiss from Dominic had left her feeling not only dazed but utterly shattered by her own response to the mere touch of his warm lips on hers. Even now, some hours later, her body still seemed to be trembling and throbbing with excitement, her senses aching with a mixture of desperate longing and thwarted desire.

Deeply ashamed of the fact that she'd made no protest—not even the mildest attempt to wriggle free from the heavy, muscular body which had been pressing her so closely to the wall—Olivia could feel her cheeks burning fiercely in the darkness. She seemed unable to prevent herself from recalling the heat of his flesh through his thin silk robe, and the clear evidence of his arousal matching her own, breathless excitement.

So it was no wonder she was finding it difficult to sleep all these hours later. Because it was Dominic, and the disastrous effect he was having on her long-dormant emotions, who clearly lay at the root of her problem.

Eventually giving up the unequal struggle, she threw back the sheet and blankets and slipped out of bed. Putting on the warm dressing gown, she padded across the carpet towards a large window on the far side of the room.

Drawing aside the heavy curtains and letting the bright moonlight flood into the room, she found herself gazing down on a formal town garden—a far cry from the rolling hills and valleys of the Kent countryside where both she and the owner of this large house had spent their childhood.

Because while it might have been ten years since she'd last seen Dominic FitzCharles, she had, in fact, known him all her life. With only a small stream dividing her family's land from that of the huge Charlbury estate and its medieval Norman castle belonging to Dominic's family, it wasn't surprising that her own father, Lord Bibury, and the elderly Earl of Tenterden, had been both close neighbours and lifelong friends.

That was in the good old days, of course. When her mother had still been alive and her father had yet to lose virtually everything he possessed.

However, in what now seemed on looking back to have been a happy, golden childhood, both Olivia and her older brother, Hugo, had been on casual, friendly terms with the three FitzCharles children: the two older sisters, Blanche and Constance, and their much younger brother, Dominic.

Whether spending the summer riding freely over the lands of the Charlbury estate, or, at Christmas time, joining the children of other local families for the traditional Boxing Day party in the old castle, Olivia couldn't remember a time when she hadn't been wildly and foolishly in love with Dominic FitzCharles.

Not that he'd ever taken any notice of her, of course. And why should he have, when she was five years younger than he was? An almost insuperable gulf when she'd been an awkward thirteen-year-old and he a glamorous, if wild young man of eighteen, roaring around the countryside in a fast sports car and already capable of breaking the hearts of so many pretty young girls.

And then, following her mother's death when Olivia was aged fourteen, her whole life had dramatically changed.

The advent of a new stepmother, Pamela, whom her father had married only a year after his first wife's death, had devastated both her brother Hugo and herself. Particularly when her stepmother had lost no time in packing Olivia off to a strict boarding school, which had left the young girl feeling utterly rejected and bitterly unhappy.

Arriving when most of the other girls had already made friends with one another, Olivia had been thoroughly miserable, rapidly becoming a difficult, turbulent teenager, seemingly determined to cause as much trouble as possible. Although if her life at school had been bad enough, her home—when she returned for the holidays—had hardly been much better.

Her father, a charming but weak man, had allowed himself to become totally dominated by the woman whom Olivia had referred to openly as her 'wicked stepmother'.

It was possible, of course, that she'd been unfair about Pamela—although the older woman's subsequent history had merely underlined her stepdaughter's sharp dislike and distrust. However, as a teenager, every issue had seemed quite clearly either black or white—with Olivia refusing to accept that there might be a point of view other than her own, and being as difficult and obstructive as

possible. And so, fighting her stepmother every inch of
the way, it had seemed as if her previously happy, secure
home had become a cold, grim battlefield.

Nevertheless, Olivia now knew that she'd been much
luckier than many children raised in a town environment.
At least she'd been able to escape from her unhappy home
life by hiding in the barns of the home farm during the
winter. While, during the summer, she'd only had to grab
a can of some fizzy drink and make up some sandwiches
before saddling up her pony, Rufus, and going off to
spend a day roaming around the countryside.

And it had been in the summer just before she'd turned
eighteen that she'd often seen the distant figure of
Dominic FitzCharles riding about the large estate which
he'd recently inherited, following his elderly father's
death the previous year.

Local gossip had been full of stories of how Dominic
was busy sowing his wild oats, both in Charlbury itself
and at Cirencester Agricultural College, where he'd been
learning up-to-date techniques of land management. In
fact, it had probably been his reputation for youthful wild
behaviour—coupled with the exciting reports of the thrill-
ingly dangerous, lethal damage he'd been causing to
young female hearts—which had added to his attraction.

And so, bitterly at odds with her stepmother, and emo-
tionally starved of love and kindness, it had been no wonder that Olivia had invested Dominic with all the mythical
attributes of a storybook hero.

Viewing him as a present-day, wicked Lord Byron,
she'd spent long hours daydreaming of how she would,
somehow, rescue him from a life of evil and dissipation.
Whereupon she would be rewarded with a chaste kiss on
her brow, the offer of his hand in marriage and then—
almost best of all—would be able to smile coolly at

Pamela's rage and fury on learning her stepdaughter was to become a countess!

Maybe if her father had been able to think of anything other than his financial problems he might have taken a closer, more concerned interest in his daughter's life. Unfortunately, left entirely to her own devices, Olivia had continued to weave her overheated, romantic fantasies about Dominic, and to worship him from afar.

But of course she hadn't been able to resist bumping into him 'accidentally on purpose'. And even now she could feel quite sick as she realised how embarrassing it must have been for him to have an adoring teenager dogging his footsteps and hanging on his every word as if it was holy writ.

However, to be fair, Dominic had never shown any sign of finding her an irritation. In fact, over that long summer, they'd fallen naturally into a regular early-morning rendezvous, when she would accompany him on her pony as he rode about his estate.

Olivia, of course, had been in seventh heaven. And, being so young, she'd been totally innocent of the various complexities of human behaviour. Totally absorbed by her *own* feelings, and her immature emotional response to her hero's dark attraction, it often seemed to her, when looking back at that hot summer, that she'd been drifting hazily in a rosy-coloured world of fantasy—light years away from reality.

So used to being treated by Dominic with the sort of casual kindness which he might have bestowed on a younger sister, she'd been blissfully ignorant of the basic facts of life. It had simply never occurred to her that he might be physically attracted to a shy girl with her wild cloud of sunstreaked, long tawny hair. Or that the burgeoning fullness of her breasts over a slim waist and gently rounded hips was providing clear evidence that she had quickly grown up to become a vibrantly attractive young woman.

Even so, nothing might have happened if, after a long, hard canter across a meadow early one morning, Dominic hadn't jumped down from his horse to inspect an old five-barred gate in a corner of the field, hanging drunkenly off a rusty hinge and clearly in need of repair.

'I'd better arrange to have that mended as soon as possible,' he called out as she rode up to join him, still breathless from urging her old pony to keep up with his much larger steed. Reining in Rufus, Olivia quickly swung her leg over the pommel of her saddle before springing down to the ground. As she did so, Dominic instinctively put up his hands to catch her, her slim figure sliding slowly down the long length of his tall, hard body.

Blushing nervously to find herself in such close proximity to her tall, handsome hero, she stared, mesmerised, at the dark hairs of his tanned muscular chest, clearly visible beneath the opennecked shirt. Quite suddenly, she became acutely conscious of his tight-fitting jeans, which appeared to hug the contours of his slim hips and powerful thighs like a second skin, her stomach clenching with a strange, unfamiliar mixture of fear and excitement.

Completely overwhelmed by her first real experience of the power of sexual magnetism, she was barely aware of his arms closing about her trembling figure as she gazed up at the grey eyes, now regarding her so intently.

'Sweet Olivia...' he murmured softly, lowering his dark head and possessing her lips in a soft, gentle kiss which left her almost swooning with joy and pleasure.

Without a thought, she instinctively raised her slim arms, winding them up around his neck as she happily surrendered to the joy and bliss of her first really adult kiss, pressing herself ardently against his hard, firm body and quivering with delight as his arms closed even tighter about her slim figure. Her emotions spun completely out of control beneath the fierce, determined possession of his lips and tongue as he savoured the inner sweetness of her mouth.

Shivering with excitement as he relaxed his grip to run his hands over the warm, soft curves of her body, she was startled when he suddenly lifted his head, swearing violently under his breath as he firmly pushed her away from him.

'Whoa!' he grated, breathing hard as he brushed a hand roughly through his dark hair, before grimly explaining to the dazed and confused girl that they must never, ever again allow themselves to get so carried away. 'You're still only seventeen, for God's sake—and completely innocent!'

'But I'm going to be eighteen in a month's time,' she protested.

'Yes, unfortunately I'm well aware of that fact,' he agreed, with a grim snort of laughter. 'But you're still far too young to go around kissing any Tom, Dick or Harry.'

'But I don't want to kiss anyone else. *Only you!*' she cried, heedless of his warning as she threw her thin arms about him, burying her face in the curve of his shoulder. 'And...and now you won't want to see me any more...' she moaned, before bursting into a storm of tears.

'Nonsense!' he murmured, gently drying her tears and promising that what he referred to as an 'unfortunate incident' wouldn't make any difference to their friendship.

Despite the fact that Dominic was scrupulously careful never to touch her again, it slowly became obvious that things would never again be the same between them. Having been given a tantalising glimpse of a world pre-

viously beyond her comprehension, Olivia now found herself awkward and tongue-tied when in his presence. And
it seemed as if he, too, had lost his normally relaxed,
careless attitude as far as she was concerned. Over the
next few weeks, he kept her at a distance, treating her
with a cool politeness which Olivia found both distressing
and highly intimidating.

With the coming of harvest time, and Dominic's need
to be more fully involved with his estate manager and the
various problems of his tenant farmers, their meetings became more infrequent, gradually dwindling, at the approach of autumn and her imminent return to school, to
an occasional wave as he passed her while driving about
his estate.

And there the matter might have ended if, on her return
home for the winter holidays, she hadn't decided to join
the local draghunt. Only to be bitterly disappointed as her
pony, Rufus, became lame after his first really hard gallop
over the frozen ground.

Determined to save her animal as much discomfort as
possible, Olivia dismounted and slowly made her way
back home.

Wishing that her brother was around to give her a
hand—instead of, as usual, avoiding his stepmother by
visiting friends in Scotland—and highly dejected at the
thought of the long, five-mile trek home—she was surprised when a large horse box drove to a halt beside her.

'Hello! What's the problem?' Dominic called out, leaping down from the cab and walking around to the back
of the vehicle.

'Rufus has gone lame. I probably shouldn't have taken
him out,' she said with a grimace of self-disgust. 'Not
when I haven't been home to exercise him regularly. I
think the hard going proved too much for the old boy.'

'I've got a mobile phone in the cab. Do you want me to phone your father, to tell him to come and pick you up?'

She shook her head, explaining that her father and stepmother were away, spending the day Christmas shopping in London.

'Well...' Dominic murmured, bending down to run his hand down over her pony's lame leg. 'There's no point in making the injury any worse. You'd better put Rufus in the horse box beside my own mount and I'll deliver you both home.'

She was worried that she might be preventing him from enjoying his own run with the hounds, but Dominic explained that his horse had cast a shoe. And, with the ground so hard and frosty, he'd decided to retire from the chase.

Grateful to be spared a long walk home, Olivia accepted his kind offer with alacrity. After loading her pony into the horse box, she jumped up into the passenger seat of the cab, chatting happily away during the short journey leading to the long, treelined drive of her family home.

Up to that point it had seemed as though their friendship was back on its old footing. However, as he helped her lead her pony out of the huge vehicle and across to the stable block, she suddenly began to feel tongue-tied and nervous, her hands all fingers and thumbs as she tried to remove the saddle and bridle.

'Here—let me do that,' he laughed, and told her to go and get some fresh hay.

'Y-yes,' she muttered nervously, almost running out of the stable block to the adjacent large barn, before sinking down onto a bale of hay for a moment as she desperately tried to pull herself together.

Although she, herself, was wearing her normal hunting

outfit of plain jodhpurs and a black coat over a simple white shirt, the sight of Dominic left her feeling weak and trembling. Elegantly clothed in long black riding boots and skintight cream jodhpurs, the white stock folded about his neck held in place by a diamond tie pin and the traditional pink coat stretched tightly across his broad shoulders, he looked absolutely magnificent.

Although she'd made a valiant effort to put him firmly out of her mind during the past three months, Olivia was shattered to find her slim figure suddenly assailed by a tidal wave of desire and longing which left her feeling shaken.

'There you are! I was wondering where you'd got to.'

Startled by the sudden sound of Dominic's voice as he entered the barn, Olivia jumped quickly to her feet.

'I...I'm sorry... I—must have been d-daydreaming...' she stuttered nervously, quickly backing away from his tall, advancing figure. 'I really don't know why— Agh!' She gave a sharp cry as she stumbled and tripped backwards over a loose bale, her fall cushioned by a soft mound of hay.

As she lay winded for a moment her face burned with embarrassment at appearing such a fool in front of her idol. However, she was relieved when he merely laughed and walked forward, holding out a hand to help pull her up onto her feet.

'Silly idiot!' he murmured, slipping an arm around her trembling figure as he picked strands of hay from her hair which—thanks to her fall and the loss of the pins holding it in a neat coil at her neck—was now tumbling down in wild confusion about her shoulders.

'I've always been mad about this colour,' he murmured softly, trailing his fingers slowly through the long, silky strands, a husky note in his voice sending shivers fizzing up and down her backbone as the arm about her waist pulled her closer to his tall, firm body.

Time seemed to be suspended. There was a strange drumming in her ears as she stared, mesmerised, up at his face, now so close to her own that she was aware of his thickly fringed dark eyelashes and the faint flush on his high cheekbones, her nostrils suddenly becoming aware of the delicious, aromatic sent of his cologne.

'I've tried to put you out of my mind...' he whispered softly, lowering his dark head towards her. 'But I don't seem to have been very successful, do I?'

It must have been her imagination, but it seemed as though, despite their clothing, she could almost feel his heart pounding in unison with her own hectic pulse-beats as she stared helplessly back up at him, dazed and hypnotised by the gleam in his deeply hooded grey eyes...

However hard she tried during the next ten years, Olivia would never be able to hide from herself the fact that, innocent and ignorant of lovemaking as she obviously was, the force of her desire and passion was every bit as strong as his.

When his lips possessed hers in a kiss of scorching intensity, her senses reeled completely out of control and she moved her body wantonly against him, provoking a deep groan as his arms tightened about her slender form.

And then they were lost, caught up in a mutual, total loss of control. However, as she would come to understand many years later, despite the raging excitement of his kisses and the thrilling caress of his hands on her body, Dominic showed considerable restraint. Gently lowering her down amidst the meadow-sweet mound of loose hay, he slowly and tenderly removed their clothes, before leading her inexperienced body from one delight to another, raising her to heights of joy and ecstasy which she could not have believed possible. While she, relishing the strength of the hard, muscular figure pressed so close to her own, ardently welcomed the final, determined possession of his lips and body.

Maybe it was the feverish intensity of her response which had overwhelmed any scruples he might have had? Certainly, they both seemed to be caught up in a frenzied longing for each other, raw passion exploding between them each and every time they managed to be alone during the following two weeks.

And then there was the traditional Boxing Day party at Charlbury Castle—and the abrupt ending to their brief love affair.

She didn't really want to go to the party at all, of course. Totally immersed in her wild love affair with Dominic, she lived only for those few, brief hours when they were alone together, deeply resenting any time which kept them apart. And therefore a strictly formal occasion—particularly one under the eagle eye of his mother—was something to be dreaded—rather than looked forward to.

Augusta, Dowager Countess of Tenterden—thin as a rake, with a ramrod back and imperious manner—was a terrifyingly arrogant woman who didn't suffer fools gladly. Known and feared throughout the district, her only soft spot appeared to be her son, Dominic, born when she'd been well over forty years of age and had virtually given up all hope of providing her husband with a son and heir to the earldom.

Moreover, since Olivia had not only grown taller but her figure had considerably developed over the past year, she knew that she had nothing suitable to wear to the party. Everything in her wardrobe was now either far too short or too tight.

Unfortunately, she was only too well aware of her father's financial difficulties. Which meant that the likelihood of him being able to afford to buy her a new party dress was very slim indeed.

'Don't be ridiculous!' her stepmother snapped when Olivia announced that she wasn't going to the Boxing Day party at Charlbury Castle. 'I've already told Augusta FitzCharles, when I met her in the village a few days ago, that you're looking forward to it. So don't let me hear any more of this nonsense,' she added irritably.

'But I haven't got *anything* to wear!' she wailed.

'Nonsense. That blue silk dress will do perfectly well.'

Oh, no, it won't! Olivia told herself glumly, glowering across the breakfast table at her stepmother. It was all right for Pamela. Why should *she* care if her stepdaughter looked a perfect fright in a dress that crushed her breasts and was far too babyish—especially when compared to what the other girls of her own age were likely to be wearing. She was going to look simply *awful*!

And she was right, Olivia told herself miserably, gazing unhappily around the Great Hall of Charlbury Castle, some days later.

Blind to the tall mullioned windows and the brilliant, jewel-like colours of the old family banners hanging from brass rods fixed high up on the vast stone walls of the old Norman castle beneath the vaulted ceiling way above her head, Olivia only had eyes for Dominic. And, as she'd feared, he was surrounded by a whole horde of smartly dressed, beautiful young girls—all of whom were much older and far more sophisticated than she was.

Maybe it wouldn't have been so bad if her older brother, Hugo, had been able to accompany her to the party. She would at least have had someone else to talk to. Not been standing here, alone and ignored, while everyone else was enjoying themselves. But her brother, who at the age of twenty was now at university, had craftily arranged to leave home the day after Christmas, going off to stay with one of his old schoolfriends.

Bitterly conscious of an occasional pitying look from the better-dressed girls, and convinced that everyone must be laughing at her old-fashioned, out of date and boring old dress, Olivia *knew* that she shouldn't have let her stepmother bully her into coming to the party tonight.

With the dancing well under way, and having only been able to have a quick, brief few words with Dominic, Olivia was standing at the far side of the room under the minstrels' gallery, wondering how soon she could hope to cadge a lift home, when a small jib door beside her was opened and Dominic quickly gripped hold of her arm, pulling her into the dark passage which lay behind.

'Come on—let's get out of here!' he said with a laugh, dragging her behind him as he strode swiftly down the passage and up a circular stone staircase, the deep indents in each stone step evidence that it had originally been a part of the ancient Norman keep.

'Where are we going?' she asked breathlessly as she scampered up the steps behind him. 'Shouldn't you be downstairs, with your guests?'

'They can do without me for a while.' He laughed again, coming to a halt on a landing, quickly pulling her into his arms and giving her a quick, brief kiss, before leading her off down yet another corridor.

With her whole world suddenly changed from deep unhappiness to great joy, Olivia would have followed him into the flames of hellfire, if necessary. But in fact his destination was considerably more prosaic—being that of his own bedroom.

'We'll be safe here,' he told her confidently, closing

the door behind them before sweeping her up in his arms and tossing her down onto a huge, ancient fourposter bed.

As always, when they were alone together, Olivia was aware of nothing but the man she loved with all her heart, the raging excitement of his kisses and the thrilling caress of his hands on her body.

They were totally absorbed with one another, and completely unaware of the passage of time, and Olivia didn't understand what was happening at first when the door was thrown open and the room echoed to a shrill cry of outrage.

Almost jumping out of her skin with fright, it took Olivia a few seconds to realise that they were no longer alone. Because there, standing in the open doorway, was the furiously angry figure of one of the girls with whom Dominic had been flirting earlier in the evening. And then, before Olivia could pull her shocked senses together, the noise of the other girl's high-pitched screech of fury brought many other guests hurrying to the scene.

The events that followed would become, over the years, a hideous blur from which she would only recall some fleeting, horrific fragments: the frantic haste with which she desperately tried to readjust her clothing, almost fainting with terror at the anger and disgust on the face of Dominic's mother, her cheeks burning with humiliation and shame as the Dowager Countess icily commanded her son to return downstairs to his guests—before ordering a servant to drive the tearful girl back to her own home, where Olivia faced far worse treatment at the hands of her stepmother.

Completely overreacting to what was, in truth, a minor incident which would be soon forgotten, Pamela went completely over the top. Claiming that she would never again dare to show her face in public, and that because of her stepdaughter's disgraceful behaviour the family had now been totally tarred by the same brush, she caused such a furore that even that mild, rather weak man Lord Bibury was persuaded to believe that his daughter was turning into the local tart. And that she must be sent far away to prevent any more embarrassment to her family.

As far as Pamela was concerned, it was obviously a perfect opportunity to get rid of her hated stepdaughter. But Olivia—treated as a social pariah and practically confined to the house in disgrace—was only concerned at receiving no word of comfort from the man with whom she was so violently in love.

While major decisions about her future were being taken, with no reference to herself, she became increasingly desperate to contact Dominic, slipping silently out of the house at night to post him letters pleading for help and rescue. Letters to which she never received any reply.

The final result of her stepmother's machinations was that Olivia was informed that her parents were not sending her back to complete her A-Levels at the end of the holidays. She was being sent, instead, to the British Institute in Florence, where she would live with a local family and learn Italian. Despite her tearful appeals, her father, for once in his life, took a firm stand. Although possibly the fact that he would save a considerable amount of money by not having to pay expensive English boarding school fees, might have had something to do with it.

Finding herself dumped in Florence in the middle of winter, Olivia had never known such misery and unhappiness. Contrary to what she'd expected, that part of Italy was freezing cold in the winter, with icy winds sweeping through the streets of the town on the banks of the River Arno.

Both the local family with whom she was staying and

the teachers at the British Institute were kind and helpful. But Olivia for a long time existed in a thick fog of bewilderment. Suddenly torn away from the only life she'd known, in England—she was equally devastated by the fact that, having written letters to Dominic giving him her Italian address, she'd never heard from him again.

Now, as she looked back down the years, she realised that it had only been the discipline of having to attend her language classes which had helped to preserve her sanity during that unhappy time. Although, as winter had slowly given way to spring and summer, she'd gradually begun to appreciate the true beauty of the city of Florence: the cradle of the Italian Renaissance, and still a mecca for those wishing to view so many outstanding works of art and architecture.

However, by the time she'd left Italy for France, and a year's cordon bleu cooking course in Paris—her stepmother having been clearly still determined to keep her well away from home—Olivia had gradually begun to recover from her broken heart.

It had, of course, taken her a long time to come to terms with the fact that the love affair which had been so central to her whole existence had meant virtually nothing to Dominic FitzCharles. He had, quite obviously, been merely enjoying himself with a casual flirtation. Despite the feelings of disillusionment and betrayal which she'd experienced at the time, Olivia now knew herself to have been nothing more than a victim of a temporary sickness. The fact that she'd once thought it to be a terminal illness only going to show how stupidly young and pathetically innocent she'd been.

For the past ten years she'd managed to push far down into the deep, subconscious depths of her mind the all too brief and fleeting moments of total happiness which she'd experienced in Dominic's arms. But now...now that they'd met once again...there seemed little she could do to keep those haunting memories from rising up to the surface of her mind.

With a heavy sigh, Olivia turned slowly away from the window and climbed back into bed. Pulling the covers up over her slim shoulders, she slowly drifted off into an uneasy, disturbed sleep, comforted by the thought that while she'd been taught a hard lesson in the past, she had indeed learnt it well.

Now that she was so much older, wiser, and well in control of her emotions, she had the satisfaction of knowing that never, ever again would she allow herself to fall a victim to Dominic's highly dangerous, dark attraction.

CHAPTER FOUR

TOSSING and turning restlessly through the night, when Olivia opened her eyes the next morning, it was to discover bright daylight flooding in through the window.

She also discovered that she wasn't alone.

'I thought you might like a cup of tea,' Dominic said, closing the door behind him before coming over to place a cup and saucer down on the bedside table.

Yawning, and feeling slightly woozy from lack of sleep, she realised that it must have been his knock on the door which had woken her.

Despite being casually dressed in a navy blue tracksuit—and clearly in need of a shave—Dominic still managed to look amazingly attractive. Although considerably less threatening than he had last night, when wearing that sexy, thin silk dressing gown.

However, there was no doubt that she'd been very tired. So maybe she had seriously overreacted to what must have been—at least by his standards—a fairly mild kiss? All the same, it was a potentially awkward situation. So it would be sensible for her to get dressed and leave the house as quickly as possible.

'Is it very late?' she asked, realising that she'd left her watch in the bathroom.

'No. It's only just after ten o'clock,' he said, gazing down at the sleepy-looking girl, her long tousled hair lying spread about her head on the pillows.

'Oh, Lord,' she muttered. 'I'm normally up long before this. I must get dressed and—'

'Relax! I've already phoned the emergency number of the department dealing with the burst water main. They tell me that it was worse than they originally thought and they are still working on the problem. It's unlikely that you'll be able to return home until much later today. Besides, it's Saturday—remember?' he added. 'So, unless you've got any urgent, vitally important appointments...?'

She yawned and shook her head.

'Well, then. I suggest you take it easy. Why not try to unwind a little? And drink your tea,' he told her firmly as he turned to leave the room.

'What about you? I mean, it was really very kind of you to put me up for the night. But I'm sure you must have arrangements of your own to see to,' she pointed out, cautiously keeping the sheet tucked up firmly under her chin. 'I certainly don't want to be a nuisance, or get in the way.'

'Nonsense!' He gave a dismissive wave of his hand. 'I've got nothing planned for today. Which is why, when I woke up to such a bright sunny day, I couldn't resist going out for a jog around the grounds of the Royal Hospital.'

'Is that where the Chelsea Pensioners live?' she asked, recalling seeing the retired soldiers, with their bright scarlet coats covered in rows of medals, at many official functions in London.

Dominic nodded. 'The old boys certainly appear to have a great life, and mostly go on to enjoy a ripe old age. So I suggest you follow their example,' he added with a grin. 'Relax. Take it easy—and drink up your tea before it gets cold.'

'Are you always this bossy first thing in the morning?' she grumbled, levering herself up against the pillows.

'Absolutely! Especially with someone who clearly doesn't know good advice when she hears it.'

'Oh, yes? And what are *you* going to do with yourself in the meantime? Go and work out in the local gym for an hour?' she queried sarcastically, gazing across the room at the tall man's lean, healthy figure.

'I sometimes think that all this keep fit philosophy has got completely out of control,' she continued gloomily, unfortunately well aware that she ought to attend her nearby leisure centre more often than she did.

He laughed. 'I'm not exactly a couch potato. But, after jogging for an hour earlier this morning, I reckon I've done enough exercise for the day. So, after making myself a pot of coffee and catching up with the latest news in the papers, I'm intending to have a leisurely shower. As you see...' he smiled sardonically as he opened the door to leave the room '...I believe in taking my own good advice!'

Deciding to ignore his 'good advice', and just have a sip of tea before getting dressed, Olivia lay back on the soft pillows for a moment, trying to come to terms with her new, rather strange relationship with Dominic.

She had, after all, been in a bit of a state when first setting eyes on him yesterday. Which wasn't surprising— given the circumstances surrounding the last time they'd seen one another. And he *had* behaved very badly. Not only in abandoning her at the first hint of trouble, all those years ago, but also never bothering to contact her again from that day to this.

And yet...a few minutes ago they'd been talking, laughing and lightly teasing one another. In fact, Dominic seemed to have been treating her as if they were just old friends, with no history of a past romance between them. Which was odd—and didn't really make sense.

Unless, of course, he'd forgotten all about that ghastly Boxing Day party? And it was *just* possible that he might have done so. Because he must have been in *far* more dodgy situations since then—if the gossip in the tabloid newspapers about his amorous escapades was to be believed! In fact, there seemed no reason why he should necessarily recall what had been, in all honesty, a very brief and quickly hushed-up local scandal.

She closed her eyes, and only realised that she must have fallen asleep when she woke up some time later to find him sitting on the bed beside her.

'Oh, heavens!' she muttered, blinking up at his handsome face. 'I really didn't mean to go back to sleep. I can't think what's happening to me…'

'You've probably been doing far too much.' He shrugged. 'Maybe this is nature's way of saying slow down?'

It was that shrug of his *bare shoulders*, which started the alarm bells ringing in her tired brain. A warning which became increasingly strident as her sleepy eyes gazed at the broad expanse of his muscular chest, liberally sprinkled with dark curly hair. From the sparkling drops of moisture still glistening on the smooth, tanned skin of his shoulders, and the damp lock of hair falling over his brow, she realised that Dominic must have only just had a shower.

The alarm bells reached a deafening crescendo as Olivia's eyes flicked nervously over the rest of his figure. That white towel tied about his lean waist and hips appeared to be the only piece of material—apart from the bedclothes, of course—separating her from his naked body.

Why on earth had she been so *stupid* as to slip off to sleep again? Did she need her head examined?

'Er—is it very late?' she asked breathlessly, before quickly turning to glance at the window, through which she could see that it still appeared to be a bright, crisp and sunny day.

'It's only about twelve o'clock. Which isn't particularly late for those wishing to spend a lazy Saturday morning in bed,' he drawled, the decided gleam in his eyes and the low, husky note in his voice making her suddenly feel extremely nervous.

'In fact, there's no need to get up at all if you don't want to,' he continued, with a slow, sexy smile. 'I can always cook you something for lunch and bring it up here on a tray.'

'You...cook me lunch?' She blinked at him in surprise, momentarily diverted from the tricky situation in which she seemed to have become embroiled. 'You must be kidding?'

'Not at all,' he told her loftily. 'My version of scrambled eggs has been much admired.'

'Oh, really?' she murmured with a grin. 'Well, I'd *never* have thought of you as a chef—let alone a maestro with the egg whisk!'

'Ah-ha! I'll have you know that I'm a man of many talents.'

'I just bet you are!' she retorted dryly, before suddenly realising that she *must* swiftly pull herself together. It was definitely time to put an end to this sort of highly dangerous flirtatious nonsense.

Because she *really* didn't like the look of that distinctly disturbing, sensual gleam in those deeply hooded eyes of his. And there was *far* too much smooth, gorgeous male flesh only inches away from her own figure.

Even if only half the things which had been written about this man were likely to be true he was still highly dangerous. In fact, she was quite certain that if anyone gave Dominic an inch he'd immediately take a yard—and anything else he could lay his hands on. On top of which, even if he was a well-known Lothario, he was also—alas!—a quite outrageously attractive one. And, let's face it, she told herself grimly, she *was* only human.

Unfortunately, if the rapidly increasing rate of her pulse and heartbeat was anything to go by, that insidious, dangerous aura of highly erotic sex appeal—which, God knows, he possessed in abundance—was *already* beginning to have a disastrous effect on her body.

So, if she didn't want to make an utter fool of herself, it was *imperative* that she escape from this situation—as quickly as possible!

'Well, I think that it's definitely time I got dressed and went home,' she said as briskly as she could, while maintaining a firm grip on the sheet.

'It's no good trying to return home. Not until they've mended that burst water main,' he pointed out, the slow, lazy smile accompanying his words practically making her toes curl. 'And that's not likely to happen until much later today. So relax...hmm?'

As he raised a hand to run his fingers through a coil of her long tawny-gold hair Olivia knew that she was in trouble. Desperately trying to ignore the shivers of sick excitement deep in her stomach, she swallowed hard, before taking a deep breath.

'Quite frankly, Dominic, I'm afraid that you're wasting your time. I'm sure there must be hundreds of glamorous women who'd give their eyeteeth to leap into bed with you, but I'm really not into this kind of heavy seduction number. OK?'

'Well...well!' he murmured. Only a slight narrowing of his grey eyes as he stared down at her with a bland expression on his face provided evidence that maybe he didn't appreciate such frank speaking.

'I must say, those "hundreds of glamorous women" certainly sound promising!' he drawled coolly. 'Unfortunately, my life seems far too hectic these days to have much time for "heavy seduction". But *do* give me their phone numbers, Olivia,' he added in a hard, mocking tone of voice. 'You never know—I might *just* be able to find a few spare moments in my busy schedule.'

'OK—OK,' she muttered hurriedly. 'I'm sorry. I obviously went a bit over the top there,' she admitted, giving him a nervous, apologetic smile as she sat up straight and looked him firmly in the eye. 'The thing is, Dominic, you don't seem to understand that I'm no longer a silly, daft eighteen-year-old—still wet behind the ears and convinced that you're the reincarnation of thrilling, wicked Lord Byron.'

'Oh, *please!*' he groaned.

'Yes, well, I'm not *too* happy about having to confess that I was such a blithering idiot, either,' she told him with a heavy sigh. 'But that was ages ago, thank goodness! Nowadays I like to think of myself as a reasonably well-adjusted, level-headed woman,' she told him earnestly. 'Definitely one who's far too sensible to play with fire—or risk getting badly burned ever again.

'So, you see...' she continued, as Dominic remained silent, gazing down at her with an unfathomable expression on his face. 'While you're obviously a good-looking, very attractive, sexy guy—and undoubtedly possess a whole list of cardinal virtues—the plain fact is that I *really* don't want to get involved with you.'

He regarded her silently for a moment. 'Well, thank you for those few kind words about my physical attributes!' he drawled, his lips twitching with amusement as he continued idly winding his fingers in her long hair. 'Certainly no one could accuse you of not being utterly blunt and to the point, could they, Olivia?'

'Well, I…I *could* have got hold of the wrong idea, of course,' she muttered, her pale cheeks flushing with embarrassment as she suddenly realised that she *might* have badly misread the situation. If so, she was going to look an utter fool if he *hadn't* been bent on seduction, wasn't she? 'I mean, you might not have had any intention of…er…'

'Having my wicked way with you…?' he murmured, clearly enjoying the sight of the deep crimson flush sweeping up over her cheeks. 'Well, whether or not I had any evil intentions, I have to say that nightdress you're wearing is an absolutely firstclass passion-killer—I can't believe it's my sister's!'

Instinctively gazing down at the Victorian-style white cotton nightgown, with its high, frilled neck and long, voluminous sleeves, Olivia raised her eyes to meet his, amazed to find herself involuntarily returning his smile of warm amusement.

'It's a perfectly sensible garment,' she told him primly.

'And highly suitable for such a "sensible" lady? I'm sure it is,' he laughed. 'But it's hardly likely to set a man's pulses racing with desire!'

'I'm glad to hear it,' she grinned, and then—with what she could only think about afterwards as careless folly—she found herself relaxing and letting go of the sheet as she raised her hands to brush the hair from her face, flicking it back behind her head.

Unfortunately, with a smooth, well-practised movement, Dominic took the opportunity to slip his bare arm around her slim figure, gently pulling her towards him as he did so.

'Oh—*come on*!' she protested, quickly placing her hands flat against his broad hairy chest and attempting to push him away. 'I've just told you that I don't want to get into this kind of nonsense. And…and what about your promise not to lay a hand on me?' she demanded breathlessly.

'Yes, I *did* make you that promise last night, didn't I?' he agreed, the husky, seductive note in his voice causing shivers to skid up and down her backbone. 'But we didn't discuss the ground rules for today. And, since you've obviously decided to cast me in the role of ''Demon Lover'', I'd hate you to be disappointed!'

'Ha-ha…very funny!' she retorted breathlessly, desperately trying to ignore the warmth of his skin and the enticing, rough texture of the curly dark hair on his chest against her palms and fingertips. 'Believe me, Dominic, there's *no way* I'm prepared to be another notch on your bedpost. Absolutely never…*ever* again!'

'You were never that—*and you know it*!' he retorted fiercely, his arms closing tighter about her body. 'For God's sake, Olivia! I can still remember every single entrancing moment of that brief time we had together.'

She gave a shrill, high-pitched laugh. 'Oh, yeah?' she jeered. 'So how come I never heard from you—from that day to this?'

'I think that's *my* line—don't you?' he growled with a sudden flash of anger, pushing her roughly away from him back onto the pillows. 'What about the fact that I never had any answer to my letters, or to my phone calls?'

'Hang on a minute! *What* phone calls and letters?' she demanded with a frown. 'From the moment I was dumped at home, after that dreadful party, to when I saw you climbing the steps outside the church yesterday, all I've ever had from you is precisely *nothing*!'

'You know very well that I tried to get in touch with you,' he ground out bitterly.

'No, I don't!' she was stung into retorting sharply. 'And there's no point in me bothering to lie about that, is there?' she added, raising her chin challengingly towards him. 'But as for you, I reckon *you* had plenty of good reasons—such as lots of other girlfriends and having to stand up to your tough old mother—for quickly dropping me like a hot potato. And that's *precisely* what you did!'

'Rubbish! You're quite wrong. It most certainly is *not* what happened,' he grated, thrusting a hand roughly through his thick dark hair.

'However, you're quite right in one respect,' he continued grimly. 'There *was* the most awful row with my mother after the guests had left the party. Although, to be fair to the old girl, a lot of what she said at the time made sense.'

He paused, gazing intently out of the window for some moments.

'There's no doubt that we were both far too young for that sort of intense, frantic love affair,' he said at last, turning back to face her. 'I also have to admit that my mother was quite right when she pointed out that I'd behaved very badly. After all, I *was* some years older than you. Which meant that I had a duty and a responsibility not to mess up your life.

'You were *very* young, Olivia.' He gave a heavy sigh. 'Only just eighteen and still at school, for heaven's sake! It was quite wrong of me to have taken advantage of such an innocent.'

There was a long silence following his words.

'I don't see how one can apportion blame in a case like ours,' she said slowly. 'While there may be a five-year difference in age between us, there's no doubt that—

however immature and silly I may have been—I did have the most *terrific* crush on you, Dominic. After all, I suppose that it does take two to tango—doesn't it?'

'It's generous of you to say so—and undoubtedly more than I deserve. However, to return to your earlier accusation, I can assure you that the bitterest argument I had with my mother was my insistence on being able to tell you—face to face—the sensible and valid reasons for putting a stop to our relationship. Until you were at least a few years older and had some experience of life.'

'But you didn't,' she said bluntly, despite being aware of the deep note of sincerity in his voice. 'You *didn't* make any attempt to see me.'

'Oh, yes, I did!' He gave a harsh bark of grim laughter. 'After phoning a few times, and being stonewalled by Pamela, I drove over to your home. Only to be told, by your damned stepmother, that you never wanted to see me again—before she slammed the door shut in my face.'

'Oh, God! That sounds just like Pamela,' Olivia muttered. 'She went completely bananas about the whole affair. In fact, I was confined to the house—until she and my father packed me off abroad to Italy, in disgrace. I'm sure no one would treat their children like that nowadays,' she added with a heavy sigh. 'It all seems so stupid, doesn't it?'

'Yes, quite crazy,' he agreed.

'But what about *my* letters?' she demanded. 'I didn't dare telephone the castle, of course. But I did write heaps of letters. Mostly very silly ones, full of angst and misery. I even wrote to you from Italy. Are you saying that you *never* received any of them?'

He shook his head. 'Not one.'

And she was forced to acknowledge that, once again,

there was no mistaking the genuine note of sincerity in his voice.

There was another long, heavy silence as they stared fixedly at one another, before Olivia said quietly, 'Your mother and my parents *must* have got together over this. Both families making quite sure that we were never able to contact one other—right?'

He nodded slowly. 'It looks like it. Because, while I regret having to say so, my mother's quite capable of going through my post. And if she also knew that you'd eventually been sent to Italy...'

'She'd have definitely known that those letters were from me,' Olivia agreed.

'So we were both fooled. You into thinking that I didn't care what happened to you. And as for me...' He shrugged, turning his dark head to stare blindly out of the window once again.

'Ah, well...that was all a long time ago, wasn't it?' he said at last, turning back to give her a cool smile. 'There's really not much point in raking up old unhappiness, is there?'

'After ten years? Absolutely not,' she agreed with a shake of her head. 'None at all.'

'OK. Well, I think we've had *quite* enough drama for one morning, don't you? In fact, we could both probably do with a stiff drink, followed by something to eat,' he added, smiling as he took hold of one of her hands, raising it to his lips for a brief moment before letting it go and rising smoothly to his feet.

'If you feel like a change of clothing, my sister left some jeans and sweaters in the wardrobe,' he said, walking across the room towards the door. 'So I'll see you downstairs in a few minutes' time,' he added, before closing the door quietly behind him.

All those revelations definitely seemed to have put him off his stroke! Olivia told herself wryly. Which was hardly surprising, since she was also feeling shattered to discover that she'd been mistaken all these years. Still, if it kept the 'Demon Lover' at bay—that could be no bad thing!

On the other hand, now she came to think about it, Dominic had not at any point actually *said* that he harboured amorous designs on her body. So maybe it had just been her overactive imagination instinctively responding to his overwhelming sex appeal which had led her to mistakenly expect a worst case scenario? If so, it was clearly time she calmed down and got a grip on herself. Starting with finding something to wear. Because her formal black velvet suit was hardly suitable attire for a casual Saturday afternoon.

Hunting through the various assortment of clothes in the wardrobe, she was so preoccupied in thinking about the past that she found herself standing fully dressed, without realising what she'd been doing.

'Watch it—it looks as if you're losing your marbles!' she muttered aloud at her reflection in the full-length mirror.

Quickly winding her long hair into a neat coil at the back of her neck, she couldn't help grimacing at the sight of herself in the baggy jeans. They were, unfortunately, far too large for her slim figure—although she had no problem with the comfortably loose, pale blue polo-necked cashmere sweater.

'That's better,' Dominic agreed some time later as she threaded one of his belts about her waist. And she was glad that she had been able to find something casual enough to match his own slim dark jeans, and navy cashmere sweater over a white opennecked shirt.

'In fact, it's nothing short of a miracle that you're able

to fit into my sister's loafers,' he added, gazing down at her feet. 'There's only one problem as far as I'm concerned…'

'Hey! What do you think you're doing?' she protested as he swiftly removed the two large tortoiseshell combs holding her hair neatly behind her head, allowing the heavy weight to tumble down her back.

He laughed. 'It seems a fair trade. You get to wear my sister's clothes,' he said, placing a tall goblet of cold, sparkling champagne in her hands, 'while I have the pleasure of enjoying the sight of your lovely long hair. Drink up!' he added with a grin, his eyes glinting with amusement as she glared up at him.

However, as she sipped her champagne there seemed no point in arguing about such a relatively unimportant subject. Especially as she discovered that, not having eaten very much at the wedding reception yesterday, she was now feeling extremely hungry. Just as she was wondering whether she should offer to cook them both a meal, Dominic appeared to be able to read her mind.

After announcing that he'd decided to spare her his culinary expertise by taking her out to lunch in a small, local French restaurant, he added, 'Their *gigot boulangère* is to die for. So hurry up and finish your drink. Because to tell you the truth, Olivia, I'm absolutely starving!'

The small French restaurant was warm and cosy, while the food proved to be every bit as good as Dominic had said it would be.

'I'm going to suggest that we leave any further discussion on our ill-fated romance until later,' he'd stated firmly as they sat down at their table.

'I'll go along with that,' she'd agreed, since his decision was clearly a sensible one.

In fact they'd chatted companionably throughout the meal, covering a whole host of subjects, and Olivia was amazed, as the waiter placed a cup of coffee in front of her, to discover just how much she'd enjoyed Dominic's company. It seemed almost unbelievable—especially when she recalled the utter dismay and nervous tension which had so suddenly overwhelmed her only yesterday.

'I'm not sure that it's ever a good idea to rehash what's happened in the past,' he was saying now, before pausing for a moment to stare at the wine glass on the table in front of him, slowly revolving its slim stem between his long, tanned fingers.

'However,' he continued slowly, 'I'm ashamed of not having made more of an effort to discover what had happened to you down the years. Which, of course, brings me neatly to the question—what *have* you been doing since we last met?'

'How long have you got?' she queried lightly.

He grinned. 'How long do you need? An hour…a day…a week…?'

'Hang on! We're only talking about ten years,' she protested with a slight laugh.

'So, why don't you start at the beginning—and go on to the end.'

'Well…it's not a very exciting story,' she warned, before telling him that after learning Italian in Florence— 'Although I'm sorry to say that my command of that language is now very rusty!'—she had then spent a year in Paris, learning to cook.

'Really?' he drawled. 'So perhaps it's just as well that I *didn't* try and cook you lunch!'

She smiled and shook her head. 'Nonsense! I love eating other people's food.'

'Hmm…' he murmured sceptically. 'OK. We've got

you as far as aged nineteen/twenty, able to speak Italian
and serve up a delicious meal. What happened next?'

'Ah…' She stared down at the table, idly stirring her
coffee for a moment. 'What happened next was that I
returned to England.'

'Did you go back to live with your parents for a while?'

She shook her head. 'No. Quite honestly, I wasn't very
welcome. Principally, I suppose, because things had become a bit tricky by then,' she said, before explaining that
her father had virtually become bankrupt and that his marriage to Pamela had clearly been on the rocks as well.

'So…' She gave another shrug. 'I stayed with various
friends for a few months, taking any odd job I could find.
And then, with Christmas approaching, I decided to become a chalet girl in Switzerland.'

'That sounds interesting!'

'It was,' Olivia agreed, before explaining that she and
her brother, Hugo, had learned to ski on family holidays
while her mother had still been alive. So the prospect of
unlimited time on the slopes had been a great inducement
to take the job.

'Hold it for a moment,' Dominic suddenly said. 'I'd
forgotten all about Hugo. What's happened to your
brother over the past years? The last I heard he was at
university.'

She nodded. 'Yes, well…Hugo got quite a good degree.
Unfortunately, a study of history isn't terrifically useful in
the job marketplace, and he sort of "lost it", if you know
what I mean.'

'It happens sometimes,' Dominic agreed quietly.

'Well, he had various other problems as well,' she admitted, before adding brightly, 'But he's now very happy,
working as a landscape gardener. Although it's probably
fair to say that it's more very small town gardens and

patios at the moment. But I'm sure he'll get some really good commissions any day now.'

'I'm sure he will,' Dominic murmured, before asking her to return to the story of her time in Switzerland. 'Was it all work? Or did you manage to have fun on the slopes?'

'I had a great time.' She grinned at him. 'Perhaps I was lucky to have really nice people renting the chalet. But, quite honestly, I thoroughly enjoyed myself. Cooking breakfast and an evening meal for eight or ten people was a breeze. And after cleaning up the place, and making a chocolate cake for tea, I could spend the rest of the day skiing up and down the mountains.'

He grinned. 'I can see that you obviously had a lot of fun. But what led you from Switzerland to arranging upper-crust weddings in London?'

'Well, it all started when I became great friends with an American chalet girl, Katherine Ross. Kate was from New York—and skied like a dream!' Olivia said, smiling to herself as she recalled the fun they'd had together.

'Basically, Kate's older sister, Robyn—a frantically busy and high-powered executive in New York—had met and fallen in love with an Englishman,' Olivia told him, going on to explain that the man's elderly parents had been too old and set in their ways to travel to the States. 'So Robyn decided to have the wedding in London—and asked Kate to organise the whole affair. When she confessed that she hadn't a clue how to go about it, I offered to help her.'

'And, that was the start of your career?'

'Well...sort of!' She grinned across the table at him. 'We made some hideous mistakes, of course. But it did prove to be a great success. And we reckoned that there must be lots of other people who, for one reason or another, needed help in organising their weddings. And we were quite right—they did.'

Relating how their business had flourished—until Kate, deciding to marry an old boyfriend, had returned to live in the States—Olivia confessed to being nervous about continuing to run the firm on her own. 'However, I'm pleased to say that, with the help of my assistant, it seems to be going very well. And that's more or less the end of the story,' she added quickly, realising that he might have found the account of her brief career rather boring.

But, while it might have been solely due to his innate good manners, Dominic appeared genuinely interested in her business.

'Yes, it has been financially successful,' she admitted, seeing no need to explain that, apart from buying her own small house—which also acted as her office—she virtually lived on a shoestring. Most of the profits from her business went to support her father—now living like a recluse in their old home—and to pay the salary of the fulltime housekeeper who looked after him.

As they rose from the table and prepared to leave the restaurant Dominic decided that, since it was a lovely sunny afternoon, it would be a good idea to collect some warm jackets from his house before going for a walk in Hyde Park.

Having run her own life for a number of years—and used to making fast, instantaneous decisions for and on her own behalf—Olivia now found it distinctly odd to be in the company of someone who automatically assumed command of any given situation.

However, to her surprise, she found it really rather restful.

Agreeing with his statement that so many of those living and working in London rarely spent time exploring the capital city, she found herself being taken to inspect the Albert Memorial, which had been restored the previous year. Then, after strolling through the park, they spent some time visiting the Serpentine Gallery, viewing the latest ultra-modern paintings and sculpture by young, *avant garde* artists.

When they finally returned to his house, Olivia turned down his suggestion that he should take her out to dinner, explaining that she really couldn't face two huge meals in one day.

'Right—there's nothing for it!' he declared with a wide grin. 'It's going to be a case of scrambled eggs in the kitchen. And don't you *dare* tell me that you don't like eggs—because it's the only dish I know how to cook.'

'Well?' he enquired some time later, as she savoured her first taste of the dish he'd just set before her. 'Is it all right?'

'Hmm...not bad—not bad at all,' she murmured slowly. 'These would seem to be very young eggs, of course—possibly laid on the north side of a farm?'

'What on earth...?'

'Oh, yes...there's definitely a slightly audacious, almost impertinent yolkiness about them.' she continued, in mocking imitation of a pseudo-wine connoisseur. 'On the other hand, I'm a little worried about the toast,' she added, struggling to keep her face straight. 'I don't feel that it's come to its full maturity as yet, and...'

'Oh—shut up, you horrible woman!' Dominic laughed.

'Actually—all joking apart—really good, deliciously soft scrambled eggs are one of the hardest things to cook,' she assured him earnestly. 'And these are really very good indeed,' she added, taking another mouthful.

'Don't worry—that's *definitely* the last time I cook anything for you.' He grinned. 'In future I'll make sure that it's *you* who wears the apron!'

'And now,' Olivia said, putting down her knife and fork at the end of the light meal, 'I really must go home. No…no, I haven't forgotten the burst water pipes,' she added quickly. 'But, having lived in the area for some time, and being fairly used to this problem, I'm almost sure that if I was to ring the Water Board they'd tell me that everything was now under control—and I'd have no problem returning to my house.'

Dominic stared at her silently for a moment, a small, ironic smile on his lips.

'I was, of course, hoping to persuade you to stay the night,' he said at last. 'However…yes, I *did* call the Water Board just before starting to cook supper. And unfortunately, my dear Olivia, it seems that you are quite right. There will be no problem if you wish to return home tonight.'

'I really have had a lovely day,' she told him later, as she came down the stairs into the large hall after changing back into her black velvet suit and white silk blouse, leaving the clothes which she'd borrowed in a neat pile in the guest bedroom.

'You've entertained me most royally, and…and although I never thought I'd say so, Dominic, it *has* been very nice to see you once again.'

'It's been a lovely day,' he agreed with a warm smile. 'Are you sure that I can't persuade you to change your mind and stay the night?'

She quickly shook her head. 'I really must go. I've so many things to do, and…' Her voice trailed lamely away as he walked towards her.

The smile slowly dying on his lips, he stood staring down at her, the glittering grey eyes beneath their heavy lids regarding her with a deep, searching intensity which left her feeling strangely weak and breathless. She tried to tear her eyes away from his, but it was as if his almost hypnotic gaze was invading her very soul.

Quite suddenly, the silence in the large hall seemed to become thick and heavy, a stifling, claustrophobic atmosphere in which the tension seemed to be mounting, second by second, until Olivia could almost feel it hammering inside her skull. He wasn't even touching her…and yet she could feel her pulse-rate quickening, heat scorching through her veins as a swift, lightning flash of sexual excitement gripped her trembling figure.

It was as if time itself had somehow become suspended. Only the quiet tick-tock of a grandfather clock, the strong, heady scent of lilies in a nearby vase, and the very faint, distant sound of traffic in the Kings Road provided any evidence of a world existing outside the soft pool of light from a nearby lamp, illuminating their two still figures.

And then, as if in slow motion, he slowly took a step forward, his hands sliding through her open velvet jacket to encircle her waist as he gently pulled her towards him.

Trapped in a strange, thick mist of dangerous languor, she was only conscious of his arms closing about her, the warmth of the strong, male body now pressed so closely to her own, shivering beneath the seductive, beguiling touch of his hands moving slowly over the soft curves of her body.

'My sweet Olivia…' he murmured, swiftly lowering his dark head to bury his face in her hair. Her senses swimming out of control, she could feel his breath fanning her ear, and the rapid thud of his heartbeat echoing her own.

'Stay with me…' he whispered huskily, before his

mouth claimed hers, possessing her lips with a kiss of such burning intensity that with a shocking suddenness raw, hot passion and raging desire seemed to explode like a volcano, deep inside her.

CHAPTER FIVE

'I THINK that's taken care of everything for the moment,' Olivia said, checking the items on the notepad in front of her before raising her head to give her assistant a tired smile. 'Did you manage to book a long white stretch limousine for the Feinstein wedding?'

'No problem. The girl working for that new luxury car hire company was very helpful,' Mo assured her, adding with a grin, 'I really love Jewish weddings. The food is spectacular—and the guests always seem to have a whale of a time!'

'I know what you mean,' Olivia agreed, leaning back in her chair and smiling at the middle-aged woman on the other side of the desk.

What she would have done over the past two years without the active help, encouragement and enthusiasm of Maureen Howard—commonly known as Mo—she had no idea. Despite the fact that the business seemed to be growing in leaps and bounds, with Olivia beginning to wonder whether she was taking on too much work, Mo had proved to be both totally reliable and a great tower of strength.

In fact, the older woman's fascinated interest in the lives of those in high society—which, Olivia privately thought, was sometimes verging on the obsessive—had surprisingly proved to be an invaluable asset. More than once, some tit-bit of gossip which Mo had gleaned from her stacks of glossy magazines had saved Olivia from becoming involved with possibly ultra-difficult or risky clients.

Never thrown by even the most outrageous requests, Mo had even managed, on one occasion, to track down an elephant! The bridal couple concerned—who'd both spent some time living and working in India—had been determined to take leave of the guests at their reception by being transported in a howdah, perched rather precariously on the back of the huge animal.

'Oh, I forgot to mention that your brother called earlier.'

'Any problems?' Olivia frowned.

'No, he sounded very cheerful,' Mo assured her quickly. 'It seems he's got a job designing someone's large garden. And, since it's just down the road from here, he wondered if you'd like to meet him for lunch next week. So I pencilled it in your diary for next Thursday. OK?'

'Yes, that's fine,' Olivia murmured, relieved that Hugo appeared to be still on the wagon, and capable of getting a job.

It was no good blaming the latter part of their childhood and the aggravating presence of their dreaded stepmother for the fact that, after studying at university, her brother had gone seriously off the rails. Children from far worse backgrounds regularly overcame all sorts of hardships and handicaps to make a real success of their lives. It was much more likely that her brother's inability to get a firm grip on life—and the fact that he was a thoroughly charming, if totally impractical man—owed more to the genes he'd inherited from his father than any childhood trauma.

Olivia had done what she could to help and support Hugo. It was she who'd bullied him into going to Alcoholics Anonymous, in an effort to cure his drinking problem. And it was she who'd paid for the extremely expensive gardening course, when he'd confessed last year that he'd always wanted to be a landscape gardener.

But it was anybody's guess just how long her brother was likely to stay on the straight and narrow, she admitted to herself with a heavy sigh. All she could do was to hope and pray for the best.

'By the way...' Olivia said, quickly snapping out of her reverie as her assistant rose to her feet, preparing to go back to her own small office. 'It looks as if there are more problems with the Chapman/Hay wedding.'

'Oh, no!' The older woman gave a theatrical groan. 'Don't tell me that those kids have broken off their engagement—*yet again*?'

'I'm afraid so,' Olivia told her with a rueful grin. 'I came into the office this morning to find a long message on the answer machine from Mrs Hay. So I think the best thing would be to put the wedding on hold for the time being.'

'It's never a dull moment as far as that particular "happy couple" are concerned.' Mo shook her head in wry amusement. 'I hope things were a lot calmer at the Turnbull wedding on Friday?'

'Yes, yes, it all went off fairly well,' she murmured, nervously fiddling with the pen on her desk as she felt her cheeks reddening under the gaze of her assistant. 'Claridge's were, as usual, marvellously efficient.'

'When I was typing up the notice of the wedding for *The Times* and the *Telegraph*, I was surprised to note that there'd been a sudden change in the best man. Where on earth did the Earl of Tenterden spring from?'

Olivia shrugged. 'I think Dominic FitzCharles was an old schoolfriend of the groom. Anyway,' she added quickly, 'he certainly saved the day by stepping in when

Mark Ryland's brother was whipped off to hospital with appendicitis. So I suppose we should all be grateful that he—'

'Hang on!' Mo exclaimed. 'Isn't he that fantastically attractive guy who's always appearing in the glossy magazines with beautiful blondes draped all over him?'

'Well…er…possibly. But—'

'I remember reading an article in the *Tatler*, I think. Anyway, it was all about the twenty most eligible bachelors in Britain. And *there he was*! Looking a billion dollars, too,' Mo exclaimed. 'Which was no surprise, when I read just how much he's worth. And as for all those glamorous, beautiful women he's been seen around with…!'

'Yes, well, I'm sure that's all very interesting.'

'And did you know that he's descended from naughty old King Charles II? On the wrong side of the blanket, of course. I think the King had it off with some Portuguese lady-in-waiting of his wife…um…what was her name…?'

'Queen Catherine of Braganza,' Olivia found herself replying, resigned to the fact that once Mo got the bit between her teeth there was no stopping her.

'Right! Anyway, the article said that the lady-in-waiting, Maria something-or-other, was a *really* sharp cookie, giving the King absolute hell until he gave his illegitimate son a title *and* a large estate. Did you know that his family still live on that estate in Kent, an amazingly romantic old Norman castle?'

'Yes,' Olivia grated.

'Well…?'

'Well—what?

'What's he like? In the flesh, I mean? Come on—give my poor old middle-aged heart a thrill!' the older woman demanded with a wide grin as Olivia remained strangely silent, staring grimfaced down at the desk in front of her. 'For instance—is he *really* as sexy as he appears in the photographs?'

'For heaven's sake, Mo! I...I was *far* too busy to take any notice of the best man,' she retorted curtly, before stating—rather more firmly than was necessary—that since they both had a busy day in front of them maybe they should get on with their work.

A slight frown creasing her brow, Mo stared down at the younger girl. It was very unusual for Olivia to even mildly lose her temper. And, now she came to think about it, her employer did seem to be looking distinctly harassed—and not at all her normal cool, calm and collected self.

'Are you feeling all right? I hope you're not catching the flu?' she asked with concern.

'No...no, I'm just a bit tired, that's all. I'm sorry to have bitten your head off just now.' Olivia gave her an apologetic smile. However, quickly deciding to change the subject, she asked Mo for the file on a well-known film star's wedding which was due to take place in two months' time.

Left alone at last, Olivia ignored the thick file on her desk as she leaned back in her chair, shutting her eyes for a moment and wishing that she could, with the wave of a magic wand, remove all trace of the past weekend from her mind.

Unfortunately, there seemed no way to prevent herself from coming to the conclusion that she was an utterly weak, feeble and pathetically susceptible female—who quite clearly needed the services of a first-class brain surgeon.

How else to explain the utterly mindless way in which

she'd so easily succumbed to Dominic's dark attraction when attempting to leave his house in Chelsea?

Continuing to lean back in her chair, there seemed little Olivia could do to prevent the scene from running through her brain like a never-ending video tape, frame by frame—as it seemed to have done continuously over the past twenty-four hours.

And what a fool she'd been to think that she'd had everything under control. So pleased with herself at the way she'd managed to remain calm and friendly while spending the day with Dominic. So confident that she simply hadn't foreseen any problem when changing her clothes before leaving his house on Saturday night. Even while she'd been walking down the stairs to see him standing in the dimly lit and silent hall Olivia had felt totally in command of the situation.

What an idiot she'd been! How incredibly foolish to imagine that she was impervious to the strong, magnetic force of his darkly sensual appeal. Because, once trapped by his arms and firmly locked in his embrace, she'd become totally lost to all sense of time and place. She'd been only aware of a desperately feverish, long-denied hunger for his touch, a compulsive need to respond to the fiercely invasive heat of his lips and tongue, blindly surrendering to the hot shivers of sexual excitement wildly zig-zagging through her trembling frame as his hands had moved enticingly over her body...

'Olivia...!' She hardly heard the hoarse, ragged groan as his mouth left hers, his lips trailing slowly down over the long curve of her throat before pressing soft kisses in the scented hollows at the base of her neck. His thickly murmured words of pleasure and delight were barely audible as his hands moved over her hips, fiercely pulling her closer to him, so that she was immediately aware of the hard strength of his arousal, an intimacy which immediately seemed to ignite an overwhelming surge of feverish desire in her own trembling body.

Trapped and enmeshed in a thick haze of highly intoxicating, erotic excitement, it was only when he turned her sideways in his arms, swiftly jerking her blouse free from the waistband of her skirt to allow him to slip his hand beneath the thin silk, sweeping it up over her soft skin to the aroused swell of her breasts, his fingers brushing enticingly over the hard, swollen nipples aching for his touch, that reality slowly began to penetrate the sensual mist of lust and desire which seemed to have her in thrall.

Instinctively she knew that she had to stop this…this mad surrender to the overwhelming force of her long-dormant emotions. She could not…must not…fall into the very same disastrous trap which had so unhappily blighted her existence in the past.

A deep surge of frantic panic and fear—together with the knowledge that she was, yet again, in grave danger of repeating one of the worst mistakes of her life—finally gave her the strength to marshal her dwindling forces and push Dominic away.

He let her go, taking a few steps back to lean against the newel post of the staircase, regarding her hurried, frantic efforts to pull herself together with an inscrutable expression on his face.

'It looks as if very little has changed between you and I—despite the passage of so many years,' he drawled, his voice heavy with irony.

That's just what I'm afraid of, she told herself wildly, her cheeks flushed as she desperately tried to avoid his gaze while frantically tucking her blouse back into the waistband of her skirt.

Sick with self-disgust at just how easily she had succumbed to his embrace, she desperately tried to concentrate on trying to do something about her long hair, falling in a long, tangled stream down her back. Unfortunately she couldn't seem to control her hands, which seemed to be shaking as if in the grip of a raging fever.

First that kiss last night and now down here, in the hall... Even *she* didn't need Dominic to point out that 'the passage of time' had done nothing—*absolutely nothing!*—to diminish his overwhelming attraction as far as she was concerned.

The silence between them had become almost unbearable when he finally cleared his throat. 'I think you and I need to have a long, serious talk, Olivia. Because it's obvious that—'

'*No!*' she gasped, quickly turning away to pick up her handbag and slinging its long handle over her shoulder. 'We really have nothing to talk about.' Keeping her back to him, she added, 'What happened in the past, was...well, that was an awfully long time ago, and I'm never going to make *that* mistake again!'

'Don't be such an idiot!' he growled, striding swiftly over the floor and catching hold of her arm, swinging her around to face him. 'What's the point of trying to fool yourself? Or me, for that matter? We both know that you wanted me a few moments ago. And it's equally obvious that I felt exactly the same way. So why deny the fact? Why deny that there's a very strong bond between us?' he demanded harshly. 'It may have remained dormant all these years. But it's clearly *still* there, ready to flare into life the moment we come anywhere near each other—right?'

'I don't care!' she gasped, as his grip tightened on her arm. 'I don't want to have anything to do with you. Dominic. You've always been bad news as far as I'm concerned. So please…please, leave me alone! Go and chase after one of your many other women,' she added defiantly. 'I'm sure that any one of them will welcome you with open arms. But not me. Because I'm simply not interested. OK?'

'What a shocking liar you've turned out to be, Olivia,' he drawled, strangely unperturbed by her harsh words. 'You can refuse to acknowledge the strong bond between us until you're blue in the face! But it's a pure waste of time. It won't make any difference,' he added with a shrug of his shoulders. 'Because it's there…it exists. It's a fact.'

'I've never heard such rubbish!'

'Which means,' he continued, completely ignoring her protest, 'I have no intention of letting you disappear out of my life again. *And that's a promise!*' he vowed in a harsh, stern voice, before swiftly lowering his head to brush his mouth over her trembling lips.

How she'd managed to twist out of his grip, dashing down the hall to wrench open the front door before running along the street as hard as she could go, was still a hazy blur in her mind.

All Olivia could recall clearly now, as she sat at her desk, her head pounding with a vicious tension headache, was quickly hailing a taxi and, as she'd thrown herself down onto the leather seat, promising herself that hell would freeze over before she had anything more to do with him.

Under *no* circumstances would she ever again make the grave mistake of going within a mile of that highly dangerous man, Dominic FitzCharles!

'Hi, darling—I'm sorry to be late,' Olivia called out, pushing her way through the tables in the small, inexpensive restaurant on Holland Park Avenue.

'It's been one damn thing after another today, I'm afraid,' she added, giving Hugo a quick kiss on the cheek before sinking down into a chair. 'How's everything with you?'

'Not bad.' He grinned, lighting up a cigarette. 'Yeah, I know.' He shrugged when she wrinkled her nose. 'But since giving up the booze I reckon I'm entitled to at least *one* vice!'

'Why not?' she said lightly, highly relieved to hear that he was still firmly on the wagon. 'Lunch is on me,' she added as a waitress approached their table.

'It's all right, Livvy. I can easily afford to buy you a meal,' he protested.

'I'm sure you can,' she assured him, although she suspected that he was not likely to be spending what little money he had on good, nutritious food. 'However, I've just landed a good job, and I feel like celebrating. So, let's have the biggest steak they've got—and all the trimmings! OK?'

'You're on!' he laughed, before making his sister happy by ordering, and then wolfing down, enough calories and protein to keep him going for some days.

'Now—tell me all about your new job,' she said, listening with interest as he enthusiastically described the work he was doing, designing a large town garden for a wealthy film producer and his wife.

'I know it isn't much of a job,' he admitted with a smile. 'But they do seem very pleased with what I've done so far, and have asked me to submit some plans for the garden at their house in the country.'

'That's brilliant!'

'Not bad!' He grinned. 'But, almost more importantly, I really love the work. I'm so much happier now than when I was trying to be a highflyer in the City—and loathing every moneygrubbing minute.'

'Well, that's what life should be all about, isn't it?' she said. 'Finding something you do well and then doing it. Although to be fair,' she added with a slight shrug, 'it's easy enough to say, but a lot harder to put into practice.'

'But what about *your* business, Livvy? Are you still having fun arranging weddings? Or have you got fed up with the whole razzmatazz by now?'

'No, I still enjoy it. Or most of the time, anyway,' she said, with a slightly weary shrug of her slim shoulders. 'This is a very busy time of the year for us, of course. So many girls want to get married on or about the fourteenth of February that the run-up to St Valentine's Day can be quite frantic!'

So used to his sister's good looks, and her cool competence at sorting out any problems in his life, Hugo suddenly realised that he might have been guilty of taking Olivia's air of calm serenity for granted. Because she was looking unusually tired and weary, with dark circles beneath her green eyes. And she'd hardly touched her food...

'Are you OK?' he asked, gazing at his sister in concern.

'Yes, of course I am!' She grinned at him. 'Just busy—that's all.'

'I think it's a bit more than that,' he said slowly. 'I've known you all our lives, Livvy—and I've got a feeling that something isn't right. So spill the beans! What's wrong?'

'Absolutely nothing—really!' she protested, before rising from the table and going over to pay the bill.

Hugo didn't believe her. But since his sister—who'd always been as stubborn as a mule—clearly didn't want to talk about the problem, there was obviously nothing he could do to help.

'Hey—I meant to ask you about our skiing holiday,' Olivia said, ordering another cup of coffee as she returned to their table.

Through thick and thin, rich and poor, she and Hugo had always managed to get together for an annual skiing holiday—even if sometimes of only a week's duration—at the end of February or the beginning of March. Which was just about the only time she could take a holiday, since her diary tended to be booked solid throughout most of the year—and especially in the summer.

'Don't forget—it's your turn to make the booking this year. So I hope you've got everything under control?'

'Oh, ye of little faith!' He grinned.

'Yeah—right!' Olivia gave a snort of sardonic laughter. 'Because I still haven't forgotten that awful *pension* in Davos—even if you have! OK...OK,' she added, as he opened his mouth to protest, 'I'll admit that the resort itself was great, and we had some of our best skiing ever. But you must agree the accommodation you found for us was simply *dreadful*!'

'Yes, well...I thought we might have a change this year. I was thinking about a trip to the United States...'

'That's a wonderful idea, but maybe a bit expensive,' she said, conscious of the fact that Hugo probably couldn't afford it. 'And it would be a very long journey, too.'

He nodded. 'I do have an alternative. How about us joining a chalet party?'

'With me acting as chief cook and bottlewasher? Forget it!' she told him with a snort of grim laughter. 'Believe me: I've been there, done that—*and* worn the T-shirt!'

Hugo shook his head. 'No—it wouldn't be a case of

you having to do anything like that. The thing is, I was
talking to an old friend from university the other day—
who's now a lawyer in the City. Apparently his parents
own a large chalet, at Courchevel. He's intending to take
a party of eight—including his sister, who'd be doing the
cooking—to stay in the chalet at the beginning of March.
What do you think of the idea?'

'Well…I don't know,' she muttered with a slight
frown. 'That area of the French Alps is a bit flashy these
days, isn't it?'

Hugo shrugged. 'Why should we care if the slopes are
littered with the jet set? The skiing is great, the accommodation is free, and all we'd have to pay for would be
our travel expenses and food. I reckon it sounds a good
deal.'

'I'll think about it, OK? Now I must dash,' she added,
after glancing quickly down at her watch.

Walking back to her office, which had gradually, over
the past few years, taken over the whole of the ground
floor of her home, Olivia found herself feeling considerably more optimistic about her brother than she had for a
long time. It really was beginning to look as if Hugo was
triumphing over his alcoholism—and he certainly looked
far healthier since giving up his work in the City and
taking to the outdoor life.

In fact, it was definitely time that she stopped trying to
wrap Hugo in cotton wool. Still, it wasn't surprising that
she'd become slightly overprotective about her brother,
she told herself defensively. He was, after all, just about
the only family that she had. Other than her father, of
course, she reminded herself quickly, her heart sinking as
she realised that she really would have to go down to her
old home next weekend, to check that he was being
looked after properly.

It was always a highly depressing visit. Lord Bibury, who seemed to be growing older and more senile with each passing day, was now a mere shadow of the tall, vital man she remembered from her early childhood.

Poor old Dad, she thought with a sudden pang of sympathy. He had neither the pleasure of grandchildren nor even the consolation of knowing that his title would pass on to the next generation. Although whether or not he fully realised that his only son was gay, she wasn't entirely sure.

And nor, to be truthful, was she. Basically because, for whatever reason, she and Hugo had never discussed the subject. And, to be honest, it was probably easier if they didn't, since she really wasn't quite sure how she felt about it. Loving her brother, and wanting him to be content, she could only hope that one day he would find someone who'd be able to bring some warmth and happiness into his life.

That's what we all need, she told herself grimly, opening her front door and walking down the small hall into her office. But as for finding it... Well, some people were just luckier than others, that was all.

Oh, no! No, she was *not* going to think about Dominic FitzCharles, she told herself with grim resolution. It was bad enough having his tall, dominant figure stalking arrogantly through her dreams night after night. She was damned if she'd allow his strong personality to invade her waking hours as well.

Especially as, thanks to him, the past week or so had been a complete nightmare.

It seemed as if her doorbell had never stopped ringing, with the delivery of one huge bouquet of flowers after another. There had been no accompanying messages, of course. Dominic was much too clever to make that mis-

take, she told herself grimly. All those years of chasing
one beautiful woman after another had clearly taught him
the danger of putting pen to paper! So there'd been only
a small envelope containing his visiting card tucked
amongst the blooms.

She'd have had the greatest pleasure in giving him a
piece of her mind—if only she'd had the opportunity to
do so. Unfortunately, while the flowers had kept coming,
there had been no other contact from him. Not until some
days had elapsed. And even then the swine had waited
until late one night—when she'd been least expecting his
phone call.

'What in the hell do you think you're doing, ringing
this late? It's almost midnight—for heaven's sake!' she'd
snapped down the phone as soon as she'd recognised his
voice, all her carefully thought out scathing remarks immediately forgotten in the heat of the moment. 'And will
you kindly *stop* sending me all those damn bouquets!'

'Don't you like receiving flowers?' he enquired in a
cool drawl.

'Of course I do,' she retorted curtly. 'But I don't
want—or need—hundreds of hothouse blooms crowding
me out of house and home,' she added through gritted
teeth.

But, almost as if enjoying adding fuel to the flames of
her fury, he merely gave a low rumble of sardonic laughter before asking when he was going to see her again.

'You're not,' she told him flatly. 'I thought I'd made
myself quite plain at our last meeting.'

'*Meeting?*' he drawled sardonically. 'Really, darling! I
don't think that "meeting" is exactly the word I'd have
used to describe the sweet warmth of your lips on mine.
Nor the way you trembled as my arms closed about you.

The delicious, velvety soft skin of your breasts beneath my fingertips, and—'

'*For God's sake, Dominic!*' she gasped, a tide of deep crimson flooding over her pale cheeks, and desperately ashamed of the erotic effect his deep, huskily voiced words were having on her body. 'You can't *possibly* say things like that! Not…not out loud…over the phone!'

'Oh, really?' he queried smoothly. 'In that case I'm more than happy to say them in person. How about having dinner with me tomorrow night?'

'What? Are you out of your mind?' she cried. 'I thought I'd made myself quite clear when I said I didn't want to see you ever again? But just in case you didn't get the message—the answer is *no*! I do *not* want to have anything to do with you, Dominic,' she added, before quickly slamming down the phone.

It rang again, almost immediately.

Cursing herself for not having switched the instrument over to her answering service, Olivia was determined to let the phone keep ringing until Dominic lost patience. But she'd either underestimated his persistence or over-estimated her own endurance. Because, finally getting to the point where she couldn't stand another moment of the highpitched, incessant noise—she snatched up the receiver.

'Olivia?'

'What is it *now*?' she demanded angrily.

Clearly not a whit troubled by her obvious fury, Dominic drawled, 'Nothing very dramatic—I just want some help with a small problem. So calm down, hmm?'

'Oh…all right.' She gave a heavy sigh of exasperation. 'What's your problem?'

'Well, it's not entirely *my* problem. But I really want to know the reason *why*—when we clearly find each other highly attractive—you are insisting on denying the fact? Why you're running away from me as fast as you can go?'

'I would have thought it was obvious!' she retorted grimly. 'All that ghastly business in the past, and...'

'There's nothing we can do about what happened years ago,' he told her quietly. 'It's too late. It's simply not possible to rewrite history—however much we might want to do so. And no one should live their lives constantly looking back over their shoulders, frightened of today because of what happened yesterday. That's a pretty spineless existence, Olivia. And I've never thought of you as a coward.'

Trembling on the edge of losing her self-control, she let a few seconds' silence pass as she struggled to pull herself together.

'I am *not* spineless!' she hissed savagely. 'And there's nothing cowardly about wanting to avoid someone who's clearly nothing but trouble! You've got hundreds of glamorous girlfriends, Dominic,' she added with a shrill, high-pitched laugh. 'So take one of them out to dinner. OK?'

'I'm not interested in any of my socalled "glamorous girlfriends", Olivia,' he told her in a hard, firm voice. 'And I might take no for an answer if I thought you really meant it. But we both know you're lying, don't we?'

'Oh, no, I'm not!' she ground out furiously. 'You're just so unbelievably arrogant and—'

'And how do I know you're not telling the truth?' he continued, taking not the slightest notice of her angry interjection. 'Because I only have to touch you and you go up in flames in my arms.'

Practically gibbering with rage, she was just taking a deep breath before letting him have it between the eyes with both barrels, when he continued, 'If it's any consolation to you, my darling Olivia, I also seem to be infected with *exactly* the same loss of control as far as *you* are concerned. So if you think you've seen the last of me...' He gave a harsh, rasping laugh. 'I did warn you the other night that you're *very* much mistaken—didn't I?'

And this time it was Dominic who slammed the phone down, before she even had a chance to reply.

Still in shock, both from the explicit way in which he'd described their response to one another and also the underlying threat in his final words, Olivia paced restlessly up and down the bedroom, her mind in a whirl of confusion and despair. Because Dominic was quite right. They *were* caught up in a tangled web of their own sensuality and sexual attraction to one another.

But *she* was also right. The only way to extricate herself from such a highly dangerous situation *had* to be the ruthless and highly sensible decision never to see him again. Because it wasn't just that she didn't trust him—and with his reputation she'd have been an idiot to do so—but she also knew that she still carried the scars of the shame and humiliation caused by their love affair in the past. Coward or not—there was no way she could *ever* face that again.

But maybe she'd been wrong to fear what now seemed to have been an empty threat? Olivia told herself now, as she settled down to do some work at her desk. It was over a week since that phone call from Dominic, following which there had been no more bouquets of flowers, nor, thankfully, had he made any further attempts to contact her.

So maybe he really *had* got the message after all? And if she found it virtually impossible to put him out of her mind, she had enough sense to know that time had a way of curing most problems. She must just try to concentrate on her work. And eventually, day by day, however long it took, the overwhelming desire and need would diminish, gradually fading away as it had done long ago.

So if that arrogant man, Dominic FitzCharles, thought there was the slightest chance that she might change her mind, he definitely had another think coming!

Dominic FitzCharles, fourteenth Earl of Tenterden, wasn't thinking of anything in particular as he absentmindedly doodled with his pen on the empty pad of paper in front of him—quite convinced that there was nothing more boring than having to sit through the official biannual meeting of his Trustees.

The Charlbury Castle Trust, originally set up by his grandfather, was admittedly a sensible way of keeping the family's assets intact, and passing them on to future generations. Unfortunately, as a life tenant receiving his income from the Trust, it would have seemed churlish—not to say ungrateful!—if he didn't at least try to look interested in the long, interminable meetings with the group of elderly City lawyers.

'…always providing that you agree with the decision, my lord?'

'Hmm?' Dominic raised his head, quickly realising that he'd been so immersed in his own thoughts that he'd failed to hear he was being asked a question. 'I'm sorry—you were saying?'

'We were merely seeking your approval, my lord, for the appointment to the board of Mr Truscott—a young, but nevertheless clever young man, highly experienced in the field of corporate taxation.'

'Oh, yes, by all means,' Dominic agreed, before suddenly wondering what would happen if, one day, he refused to ratify any of his Trustees' decisions. It was rather depressing to realise that they would probably just smile rather indulgently at him before briskly proceeding to take no notice of his wishes whatsoever.

'Thank goodness that's over!' he said with a sigh of relief as he climbed into the driving seat of the Range Rover, slamming the door shut and doing up his seat-belt.

'You'll be glad to hear that it's time to go home, Duke,' he added, turning to grin at the black Labrador, who'd been sitting on the passenger seat, patiently waiting for his master to join him.

A Christmas present from his favourite sister, Connie— who now lived thousands of miles away, in New York— the dog had immediately, even as a small puppy, firmly attached himself to his new master.

It was Connie who'd insisted on calling the animal Duke—because, as she'd said, 'It will do you good, Dominic, to have someone of higher rank around the place!' However, on her last visit home, Connie had wondered whether she ought to have called the dog Shadow. Because even nowadays he would still insist on accompanying her brother whenever possible.

Switching on the ignition, Dominic hesitated for a moment. 'What do you reckon?' he asked Duke, who was gazing up at him with large brown eyes. 'Do you think it would be a mistake to make a detour via Holland Park on our way home?

'Yes...perhaps you're right,' he said, after a moment's thought. 'I think I'd better resist the temptation and try to come up with a slightly more subtle approach instead,' he added, grinning down at the dog, before letting in the clutch and driving slowly through the crowded streets of the City of London.

Finding himself caught up in the rush-hour traffic, firmly stalled on the approach to the Tower of London and its bridge over the river Thames—the route leading

through South London back to his home in Kent—
Dominic found he had plenty of time in which to consider
his problem. Leaning back in the driver's seat, he con-
centrated on recalling the long conversation between himself and Olivia when he'd taken her out to lunch in the
small French restaurant around the corner from his house
in Chelsea.

Always having regarded himself as a reasonably cool,
laidback sort of man, with a fairly cynical view of life,
Dominic was used to solving most problems in front of
him. Which was why he now found the current state of
his relationship with Olivia Johnson extremely disturbing.

There *had* to be some way of getting through to the
woman who—God knows why—was responsible for
causing him considerable internal havoc and thoroughly
upsetting his normally well-ordered life. He couldn't remember any female of his acquaintance *ever* giving him
such a hard time. In fact, if he had any sense at all,
Dominic knew that he'd be well advised to put all thought
of Olivia well behind him. She'd caused enough trouble
in his life once already. Besides, he was a busy man who
ran his diary with iron control, on the principle of 'business first—pleasure second'. So why he'd allowed that
woman to get in under his skin he had absolutely no idea!

And then, as the traffic still showed no sign of moving
forward, he suddenly recalled to mind a brief sentence or
two amongst many of the things they'd discussed at lunch
that day.

Clicking his teeth with annoyance at not having thought
of it before, he quickly punched some numbers into the
mobile phone attached to his dashboard.

'That's great, Bill,' Dominic murmured, his fingers
beating an impatient tattoo on the wheel as he forced him-

self to listen to what his old friend had been doing since
they'd last been in touch with one another.

'By the way, Bill,' he finally managed to say in a casual
voice. 'You remember that small problem with one of
your employees whom you suspected of industrial espio-
nage? I wonder if you still have the name and address of
the investigator who sorted out the problem for you? Oh,
you have…that's great!'

Dominic grinned, leaning over and taking a small pad
and pencil from the glove box. Quickly scribbling down
the name and telephone number of the man concerned, he
said 'Thanks, Bill—I'll be in touch,' before quickly ter-
minating the call and dialling another number.

'Ah, Mr Foster,' he was saying a few moments later.
'We haven't met, of course, but I believe you did some
invaluable work for a friend of mine, Bill Andrews. And
I was wondering if you could help me to solve a small
problem…'

By the time he'd driven over Tower Bridge, and was
well on his way down the Old Kent Road, Dominic was
feeling decidedly more cheerful and optimistic.

He'd told Olivia that she was much mistaken if she
thought she'd seen the last of him. And now, he told himself, his lips twisted in a small smile of satisfaction, it
looked as though she should have remembered his family
motto: *Quod Promitto Perficio*—What I Promise—I Will
Carry Out!

CHAPTER SIX

STARING out of the window as the train sped through the open countryside towards the snowcapped peaks of the French Alps, Olivia gave a heavy sigh. Why was it that just lately it seemed as if her whole existence had been turned upside down?

As far as she was concerned, the disruption of her normally calm, well-ordered life all stemmed from the sudden, dramatic reappearance of Dominic FitzCharles.

To be strictly honest, it was now well over a month since her last contact with the awful man. However, Olivia had no doubt that he was the root cause of the bad dreams and sleepless nights from which she'd been suffering ever since first setting eyes on him at Mark and Sarah Ryland's wedding.

And now it was Hugo who'd inadvertently caused even more disruption in her life.

Olivia gave another heavy sigh, leaning back in her seat in the first-class section of the Eurostar train.

It wasn't really fair to blame her brother. He had, after all, been offered the chance of a lifetime. A fact which she'd instantly recognised when he'd rung her in a state of great excitement, some weeks ago, with the news that he would be forced to cancel his skiing holiday—after they'd finally decided to join the chalet party at Courchevel in the French Alps.

'I'm really sorry about this,' he told her down the phone. 'But when I got offered this job, out of the blue,

I simply *couldn't* afford to turn it down. You do see that, Livvy, don't you?'

'Yes…yes, of course I do,' she muttered, struggling to keep the disappointment out of her voice. 'It's not the end of the world. I can always have a holiday later on, in the autumn.'

'Hang on! *I'm* the one who's having to cancel the trip—not you.'

Olivia shrugged her slim shoulders. 'I really don't think that I want to go on holiday with a bunch of strangers. Especially if most of them have known each other for a long time. You must see that it's likely to be a bit awkward,' she added as he gave a snort of irritation down the phone.

'No, of course I don't see it!' her brother retorted. 'Why on earth are you being such a drip? I mean, you haven't *got* to have anything to do with the others if you don't want to—right?'

'Yes, I know. But…'

'Frankly, I reckon you'd be mad not to go,' he said firmly. 'Apparently the chalet is simply enormous, and very comfortable. And while I've never been there, John Graham—whose parents own the place—tells me that it's apparently in the Jardin Alpin sector of Courchevel, known locally as "Millionaire's Row". Which can't be bad!'

'Well…'

'John will, of course, be getting in touch with you,' her brother continued impatiently. 'And I understand that if he can't give you a room on your own, he'll make sure that you share a bedroom with his sister, Charlotte. And I can vouch for the fact that she's a really nice girl.'

'Hmm…' Olivia murmured cautiously.

'Besides,' her brother was saying, 'why should you

care—even if you decide that you simply hate the other members of the party? The place might have a bit of a jet set image, but it's also got lots of seriously challenging skiing—with some of the best off-piste powder runs in the French Alps.'

And so, after her brother's friend, John Graham, had been in touch with her, Olivia had eventually decided to join the skiing party which he was organising on her own.

'It's going to be a fairly easygoing, relaxed bunch of old friends,' John had told her at their brief, hurried meeting in a bar near the Law Courts.

'My sister's quite a good cook. But if anyone can't stand Charlotte's version of *haute cuisine* there's no need to worry. Luckily there are plenty of really good restaurants nearby!' he'd added with an infectious rumble of laughter.

Deciding that she liked her brother's friend, whom it turned out she had met before—very briefly, without catching his name—since he'd been a guest at Mark and Sarah Ryland's wedding, Olivia had felt a good deal more optimistic about the holiday by the time they had gone on to discuss her transport arrangements.

'My sister and I are going to be driving out to the chalet. My parents have one or two small pieces of furniture and some linen which they want us to take with us to France,' he'd explained, before adding, 'Unfortunately, that means we won't have enough room in the vehicle to offer you a lift.

'Quite frankly, Olivia,' he'd continued, after a moment's thought, 'it might not be a bad idea to take the Eurostar. It runs from Waterloo Station about nine o'clock on a Saturday morning, arriving at Moutiers about eight hours later. It's a dead simple journey, and virtually hassle-free.'

It had obviously been worthwhile finding the time to meet up with one another, because John Graham was obviously a very nice man, and clearly fond of Hugo. And after he'd assured her that there would be someone to pick her up from the rail station at Moutiers, for the forty-minute journey by car to the chalet, Olivia had begun to believe that maybe the holiday wasn't going to be the disaster she'd feared, after all.

But, after arriving in Moutiers, and just as she was stamping her feet to keep warm on the cold, icy ground, Olivia suddenly realised that she'd made one major and possibly disastrous mistake.

Amidst all the arrangements for her holiday, why...*why* hadn't she asked John Graham how she was supposed to recognise the person meeting her at the station. Or, indeed, how *they* would recognise her?

Oh, Lord! It was going to take *ages* for all these other people milling about her to find their seats in the many coaches and taxis parked outside the station. So the chance of any one person being able to spot her—or vice versa—was likely to be very slim indeed.

Cursing herself for having been such a fool, Olivia was just deciding that it might be sensible to go and have a cup of coffee in a nearby café, until the crowd had thinned out somewhat, when she nearly jumped out of her skin at the sound of her name.

And much, *much* worse was the fact that she instantly recognised the voice!

'*Dominic!* What on earth are you doing here?' she gasped, her eyes widening in shock at the sight of his tall, dark figure striding towards her.

'I can't *believe* this is happening to me,' Olivia wailed some ten minutes later as, having stowed her skis and luggage in the back of his large blue Range Rover,

Dominic settled into the driving seat and switched on the engine. 'I just *can't* believe it!'

'What can't you believe?' he asked coolly as she fumbled with the straps of her seat-belt.

'The fact I was hoping to have a nice, quiet holiday. And then *you* suddenly appear from nowhere—like some evil magician in a pantomime,' she retorted grimly. 'The only thing that appears to be lacking is that you're not trailing the usual cloud of poisonous green smoke!'

'Thank you for those few kind words,' he murmured sardonically. 'Really, Olivia! I've never known a woman who gives me so much hassle as you do!'

'And you've known *so many* women—haven't you?' she snapped, still fighting with her seat-belt, and swearing violently under her breath.

There was a long silence as her caustic, scathing words echoed around the enclosed space of the vehicle. A moment later she found her chin gripped firmly by his hand as he turned her face towards him, a grim expression in his hard grey eyes.

'I'm quite willing to give you a lift to the chalet—and explain how and why I'm here in France while doing so. But I'm *not* prepared to put up with a petulant, tiresome display of rudeness and bad manners,' he told her bluntly.

'So it's entirely up to you, Olivia. You've got a clear choice. You can decide to behave like a polite member of society. Or you can get out of the vehicle and either make your own way to the chalet or return to England, if you so wish. Which is it to be?'

Her cheeks burning, Olivia's eyes fell nervously away from his hard, steely gaze. Unfortunately, Dominic was right. She *had* been guilty of behaving like a spoilt child.

'Well?'

'I...I'm ashamed to say that you're quite right,' she

admitted in a small voice. 'I'm sorry, it's just been a bit of a shock, I'm afraid...' she added, suddenly feeling intimidated by the dynamic, masculine presence of the man sitting so close to her. She could almost physically feel the force and energy flowing from his strong, broad-shouldered body, the harsh glint in the eyes boring down into her own.

She instinctively flinched as his dark head seemed to move nearer to her. So close that her senses became instantly and acutely aware of the aromatic scent of his cologne, the light touch of his breath fanning her cheek, and the tension in the long, tanned fingers still firmly gripping her chin. Dazed, she found herself staring, mesmerised, up at the mouth, only inches away from her own, a sudden quivering excitement flashing like liquid fire through her veins.

And then the hand firmly gripping her jaw seemed to relax, the harsh, stormy glare in his eyes gradually softening as his lips curved into a slightly ironic smile.

'I think we'd better do up your seat-belt, don't you?' he murmured, leaning across to take the steel buckle from her trembling fingers, firmly clicking it shut before he set the car in motion.

Olivia turned her head away, to stare blindly out of the window at the darkness beyond the well-lit road. She'd never been in this part of the French Alps before. If her mind hadn't been in such a chaotic whirl, she knew that she'd be in a better position to appreciate the sight of silvery-white snow, glistening as it drifted slowly down past the car headlights.

She must...*she really must* try to calm down and get her act together, Olivia told herself desperately, still feeling dazed and totally out of her depth at the speed of events over which she seemed to have no control.

Glancing sideways through her lashes at Dominic's austere, hawk-like profile, she saw that he was clearly concentrating on the road, his lips clamped together in a hard line, with his hands firmly gripping the wheel in front of him.

So it didn't look as if she had any choice. She was going to have to make an effort—to eat humble pie, if necessary, even if it choked her—in an attempt to try and dispel the tense atmosphere within the vehicle. Because the sooner she discovered what was *really* going on, the sooner she'd be able to make up her mind what to do about the situation.

'I'm sorry if I didn't behave very well just now,' she told him with a sigh. 'I had to get up very early this morning, to catch the train at Waterloo. And after the long eight-hour journey...well, I expect I'm just tired, that's all.'

'Yes, well...maybe I should have made allowance for that fact and not been quite so tough on you,' he said, turning to give her a quick, brief smile. 'We do seem to rub each other up the wrong way at times, don't we,' he added wryly, turning back to concentrate on his driving once again. 'But if we're going to be spending the next two weeks in each other's company, it might be a good idea to call a truce, hmm?'

Two weeks? Olivia knew that she was tired and weary from the journey. But she simply couldn't begin to think of how she was going to cope with this man's company for *two whole weeks*!

Even attempting to try and work out the complicated, involved feelings she had for him was almost beyond her at the moment. And why, when she'd always prided herself on her calm, serene acceptance of life, she should have felt impelled by an instinctive gut reaction to mentally hit out at the tall figure now sitting beside her, she had absolutely no idea.

'It does seem to be an amazing coincidence, doesn't it? I mean…that you're not only here, at the same time as myself, but also apparently staying in the same chalet,' she said quietly.

'Yes, I can see that it might strike you as a bit odd,' he drawled, his concentration clearly focused on the traffic and the road ahead of him.

Damn right, it's odd! Olivia told herself grimly. She was willing to accept that strange coincidences could undoubtedly happen in life. But this was ridiculous!

'Would you like to tell me more about this "odd" situation?' she asked.

'In a moment,' he muttered, adjusting the rate of his windscreen wipers as the snow began falling even faster.

'Right…' he said at last, still keeping his eyes focused on the road. 'It isn't really quite so strange as it might seem. I was at school and have remained friends with both John Graham and another friend who's staying at the chalet with his new wife. So, when John had an unexpected, last-minute vacancy in his numbers for the chalet party, I agreed to make up the party.'

'Hmm…' Olivia murmured. It didn't sound totally unreasonable. But, all the same, she had a distinct feeling that there was a lot more lying behind the ultra-simple explanation which she'd just been given. It was simply too pat.

'So you didn't know that it was my brother who couldn't make it and that I was still coming?' she persisted.

'John may have mentioned something to that effect,' he admitted after a small pause.

'I thought so…' she muttered, desperately wishing that

she wasn't feeling quite so travel-weary as she tried to pummel her tired brain into thinking through the consequences of being here with Dominic. How long have you been here, in France?'

He shrugged. 'Only marginally longer than you, yourself,' he told her, before reaching forward to the glove compartment and extracting a map which he placed on her lap. 'You're going to have to be in charge of directions—so I hope you're good at map-reading, Olivia?'

'You mean...' She turned to gaze at him in bewilderment.

'I mean that I don't know any more about this chalet—or some of the people who'll be staying there—than you do,' he said, explaining that he'd only left London yesterday, travelling through to France via the Channel Tunnel and taking the A26 autoroute as far as Reims, where he'd spent last night in a warm, comfortable hotel.

'But—but why choose to take that route?' she frowned.

'I've been skiing at least once or twice a year since as long as I can remember. Although for the past few years I've mostly chosen to ski in America and Canada. Principally because anyone who's experienced Gatwick or Geneva airports on a Saturday in either February or March will have got fed up with the sheer number of crowds. Not to mention all the hassle and the delays in trying to reach their destinations in Europe,' he added, before telling her to hurry up and get the map open at the right place, because he was soon going to be asking her for directions.

'So, when I'd joined John Graham's chalet party, I decided to travel by car,' he continued as she wrestled with the large map, trying to fold it down into manageable proportions. 'Quite apart from anything else, I reckon it's always useful to have transport available—especially when on holiday in an unknown location.'

Having managed to fold the map down into a reasonable size, and concentrating on locating the direction they would need to take, Olivia was struck by a sudden thought.

'Just a minute…' she said, turning to stare at him with a frown. 'If you knew from John Graham that I was coming out at exactly the same time as yourself, why didn't you let me know that you'd be joining the party? I mean, you could have offered me a lift!'

'*Ah!* Now that really *is* the most interesting question you've asked so far!' he drawled, a distinct note of amusement in his voice.

'Well?'

He shrugged. 'Let's put it this way, Olivia. If I *had* contacted you with the information that we'd be spending the next two weeks together, and asked you whether you would like a lift with me, to the chalet at Courchevel, what would your response have been?'

'I'd have immediately cancelled the holiday,' she told him without a moment's hesitation.

He gave a low rumble of sardonic laughter. 'It didn't take me more than a few seconds to come to *exactly* the same conclusion,' he agreed. 'And, since I realised that you must have had a tiring year, and needed a relaxing holiday, it seemed the very least I could do not to disrupt your arrangements.'

'How *very* thoughtful of you!' she muttered through gritted teeth, turning to cast a glance of loathing at his arrogant, handsome profile, her frustration and fury at the situation in which she found herself inflamed by the sight of his lips twitching with amusement.

It took some time, of course, but Olivia gradually managed to bring her seething anger at the discovery of just how easily she'd been manipulated by the foul man sitting beside her under some sort of control. However, there was clearly nothing to be gained by having a rip-roaring quarrel with Dominic. Especially as the driving conditions were getting more difficult. And she had a responsibility, as his passenger, not to distract the man's attention from the road in front of him.

Besides, there was absolutely nothing she could do about the situation at the moment. If, after a good night's sleep, she decided that she either hated the chalet—or the other members of the group, whom she had yet to meet— there was nothing to stop her getting a taxi or hitching a lift to the nearest airport and flying back home to London. So, however furious she might be with Dominic—and she was, in fact, extremely cross—she was clearly going to have to wait for a better time and place to give him a piece of her mind.

However, she soon realised that it was just as well she had decided to be sensible, and not have a row with Dominic, since reading the map was proving very difficult, and she needed his help in making sense of the terrain. Particularly since there appeared to be at least three sections of Courchevel in the Trois Vallées.

'Our destination is the one labelled Courchevel 1850,' he told her, explaining that the numbers referred to the height in metres, with Courchevel 1650 and 1550 being lower down the mountain.

'Talk about complicated!' she muttered, peering down at the map in front of her.

'You're so right,' he agreed, and for almost the first time that day they seemed to be in complete accord with one another. A situation which continued until he at last brought them to a halt outside their destination: a large

Alpine chalet, with its roof almost sweeping down to the ground.

It was only when Dominic peered through the windscreen, with his headlamps clearly illuminating a large sign over the front door of the building, that the fragile harmony which had briefly existed between them looked as if it might be put in jeopardy.

'I don't believe it!' he muttered, before throwing back his head and roaring with laughter.

Following his gaze, she saw, etched in thick black letters, a large sign saying 'Mon Coeur'.

'I don't see what's so funny?' she shrugged, wondering what sort of people would choose to call their house by such an outlandish and rather silly name.

'Well, I find it very…er…amusing—under our present circumstances,' he told her with another deep rumble of ironic laughter, before opening his door and jumping down into the snow.

'Welcome, my darling Olivia,' he declared, coming around to open the passenger door for her with a theatrical flourish. 'Welcome to "My Heart"!'

After a good night's sleep, Olivia was feeling far more her usual self when she finally opened her eyes the next morning.

Lying back against the pillows, she gazed sleepily around at the large bedroom, with a door leading to the sumptuously appointed *en suite* bathroom, before noting that the bed on the other side of the room was empty. Charlotte Graham was clearly already up, and downstairs in the kitchen cooking breakfast.

A small smile playing around her lips, Olivia recalled the days when she had been one of those hard-working creatures—a chalet girl. That wasn't precisely Charlotte's role during this holiday, of course. However, when told that John Graham's sister had volunteered to do the shopping and cooking for the chalet party, Olivia had known all about the amount of work involved. As she remembered so well, the girl would have to rise before anyone else to make sure that breakfast was ready and waiting before the chalet's occupants hit the slopes.

Well, that's not my job this time—thank goodness! she told herself with a grin, continuing to lie in the comfortable bed while she thought back to the arrival of herself and Dominic last night.

Really, now that she came to think about it, the day had comprised one startling surprise after another. Because no sooner had they entered the warmth and comfort of just about the most luxurious chalet she'd ever come across than Olivia had been utterly amazed to find herself being welcomed by the smiling faces of Mark and Sarah Ryland.

'What in the heck are the two of you doing here?' she'd gasped in surprise. 'I thought you were going on to Hong Kong after your honeymoon?'

'So did we!' Sarah had laughed. 'But the bank Mark works for suddenly transferred him back to London. Since there's six weeks before he has to take up his new post, we decided to accept John's invitation to join everyone here, at the chalet!'

After casting a grim, tight-lipped glance at Dominic, who, from the laughter gleaming in his grey eyes, had clearly known all along that the Rylands would be joining the party, Olivia had realised that she felt a lot happier at having at least two friends in the party.

But she hadn't been given an opportunity to have a few, sharp words with Dominic, as she'd quickly found a glass of wine being pressed into her hand before being introduced to the other guests.

There had been a tall, fairhaired man called Julian—she hadn't caught his last name—who'd remained virtually silent throughout the evening. In complete contrast to his girlfriend, Tracy, a tall and slim, spectacularly beautiful girl, whose lowcut black sweater had left no one in any doubt that she possessed a spectacular figure.

With her wonderfully smooth, tanned skin, and a mass of flamboyant, deep red hair, Tracy—who was apparently an actress, currently 'resting' while hoping for a small part in a film—had looked absolutely stunning. A complete contrast to John's sister, Charlotte.

Plump and jolly, her snub nose dusted by a sprinkling of freckles beneath her short chestnut-brown, curly hair, Charlotte was clearly a 'jolly hockey sticks' sort of girl, leaping around like a puppy, and doing her best to make sure that everyone had had enough to eat and drink.

Unfortunately, by the end of the evening, Olivia had come to the conclusion that Charlotte—nice, sweet girl though she might be—was clearly accident-prone. And it had been the way that Tracy had reacted to the number of small accidents—such as Charlotte tripping over a carpet, dropping a glass loudly in the kitchen and knocking a glass of red wine all over the white tablecloth—which had led Olivia to think that she and the redhead weren't likely to become good friends.

However, although that thought had originally only hovered vaguely in her mind, it was the way the other girl had reacted to Olivia, herself, which had possibly prompted her own instinctive dislike. Because, for some reason she had yet to fathom, Tracy was clearly not at all pleased by Olivia's arrival at the chalet.

What had prompted the other girl's barely concealed

antagonism, she had no idea. And, quite honestly, she'd
been too tired last night to particularly care one way or
the other. However, since she was going to be out skiing
every day, with any luck she wouldn't have to see too
much of Tracy—who was clearly far more interested in
the *après-ski* life than taking any form of healthy exercise.

Quite what she was going to do about the state of her
relationship with Dominic was still something which
Olivia hadn't really sorted out. For one thing, she really
had been very tired, last night—deciding to retire to the
bedroom she shared with Charlotte immediately after supper. There had been no point in trying to sit down and
cudgel her weary brain when she'd obviously needed a
good night's sleep before sorting out the problem.

It was all going to depend, of course, on how much
everyone 'did their own thing'. If it seemed likely that
she'd be seeing very little of Dominic then there seemed
no reason why she shouldn't be able to calm down and
enjoy her holiday. But the only way to find that out was
to get up, get dressed and discover—probably from
Sarah—exactly how the setup at the chalet was likely to
pan out.

Since she was planning to spend the morning organising her ski-lift pass and generally exploring the town,
Olivia had a quick shower in the luxurious bathroom, before putting on a pair of slimcut warm black trousers, a
black long-sleeved silk shirt and a thick-knit emerald-
green sweater.

Entering the large dining room, Olivia was relieved to
note that she wasn't the last to rise, since, although most
of the party were sitting around the table, Dominic and
John Graham appeared to be missing.

And then, as she walked slowly over to the table, she

noticed the anxious-looking expressions on the faces of her companions, and the general air of gloom.

'What's wrong?' she asked quietly, sinking down into the chair next to Sarah.

'John and Dominic have taken Charlotte off to hospital,' the other girl told her. 'Nobody seems to know *exactly* what happened. But apparently Charlotte went out this morning, to get something which she'd left in her brother's car, before unfortunately slipping on a patch of ice and breaking her leg.'

'Oh, how awful!' Olivia exclaimed with concern.

Sarah nodded. 'Luckily, it seems that Dominic was up early, and heard the girl's cry for help. So he quickly roused John, before driving both Charlotte and her brother to the local hospital.'

'It's damned bad luck,' Mark said from the other side of the table. 'Poor Charlotte! What a rotten thing to happen on virtually the first day of her holiday.'

There was a general murmur of agreement around the table, apart from Tracy, who was leaning back in her chair and looking thoroughly disgruntled.

'Well, I suppose one has to feel sorry for the girl,' she said with a shrug. 'But, all the same, anyone could see that clumsy idiot was just an accident waiting to happen!'

The fact that there was a certain amount of truth in what the redheaded girl had said didn't make her words any more palatable to the rest of the company.

'I think that that's a foul thing to say,' Sarah protested, glaring angrily at Tracy. It was clearly only Mark's intervention—quickly reaching forward to catch hold of his wife's hand, and accompanying his gesture with a quick warning frown—that prevented her from saying any more.

Mark had been quite right, Olivia decided. As much as she was beginning to actively dislike Tracy, there was no doubt that they were all going to have to get on with one another for the next two weeks. So any quarrels or arguments at the beginning of the holiday were best avoided.

'I think we could all do with a strong cup of coffee, don't you?' Olivia said, and a murmured chorus of approval greeted her words as she rose and went next door to explore the kitchen.

Poor Charlotte clearly hadn't started getting breakfast ready before being overtaken by her accident, which meant that it took Olivia some time to hunt through the various cupboards, trying to locate both the coffee and a large cafetière. Finally managing to assemble everything on a tray, she was just about to carry it into the dining room when she heard the sound of a door banging and raised voices next door.

Tray in hand, she paused in the open doorway of the kitchen, staring across the room to where the solitary figure of Dominic was clearly giving everyone a brief, up-to-date report on Charlotte's condition.

'The good news is that she hasn't broken a leg,' he was saying, his words being greeted by a buzz of relief. 'However, I'm sorry to have to tell you,' he added with a grimace and a brief shake of his dark head, 'that Charlotte *has* got a real problem with her ankle. I'm not sure whether it's a simple break or a compound fracture, because they're still taking a series of X-rays,' he explained. 'But there are so many small bones in that part of the body—and it's so important that they're set correctly—that John has decided to stay on at the hospital to be with his sister, until the arrival of a top local surgeon.'

Unable to answer the battery of questions being hurled at him by the other members of the party, Dominic could only shake his head. 'I really don't know how long the poor girl's going to be in hospital. But almost certainly for the next few days. And even when she returns back here to the chalet we'll all have to make sure that she's properly looked after, and doesn't put any weight on that ankle.'

The long silence following his possibly accurate but gloomy forecast was finally broken by Tracy's high-pitched, whining voice.

'It's all very well feeling sorry for that stupid girl, Charlotte. But what *I* want to know is—just *who* is now going to do the cooking?'

CHAPTER SEVEN

So—WHAT else is new? Olivia thought glumly, standing at the sink of the kitchen peeling a mound of potatoes.

From the moment that unpleasant girl, Tracy, had self-ishly demanded to know where her next meal was coming from, Olivia had immediately seen the whole rotten scenario stretching out ahead of her.

Indeed, she'd hardly needed to hear Sarah's breathless protest, 'Oh, *please* don't ask me to do the cooking. I've only just learned how to boil an egg!' to know that she was trapped, doomed to once again put on an apron and assume the role of chief cook and bottle-washer at the chalet Mon Coeur!

Not that she'd gone down without a fight, of course.

With Tracy confirming her worst fears by flatly refusing to even enter the kitchen, let alone wield a wooden spoon, Olivia had walked forward to put the tray down on the table before placing her hands on her hips and sternly regarding the remaining members of the chalet party.

'I've got no problem with a male chef,' she'd stated firmly. 'So, any offers to do the cooking from you men?'

But Mark, rolling his eyes in horror, had quickly protested that he was no better versed in the art of food preparation than his new wife. While Julian, who was clearly a stranger to any form of the spoken word, had gazed mutely up at her before slowly shaking his head.

As for the third member of the male sex? Well, to give the devil his due, Dominic—the one person in the room aware of her culinary expertise—had chosen to keep that knowledge to himself. Only the amusement glinting in his grey eyes beneath their heavy lids had betrayed his knowledge of the dilemma she'd faced.

'My dear Olivia,' he'd drawled smoothly. 'I am, of course, anxious to do what I can to help. Especially since I'm sure you *can't* have forgotten my wonderful scrambled eggs?'

Unable to prevent a hectic flush sweeping over her cheeks at the memory of the evening she'd spent in his house, Olivia glared across the table at him as he turned to the other members of the house party.

'Believe me: my scrambled eggs are a real *pièce de résistance*,' he'd told them, waving a hand theatrically in the air. 'Unfortunately…it is the *only* dish I know how to cook. However, if no one minds eating it for breakfast, lunch and dinner, every day for the next two weeks—then of course I'm quite willing to…'

'Thanks, Dominic—but I think we'd prefer *not* to take up your kind offer!' Mark had laughed.

Eventually, of course, and realising that she had no choice in the matter, Olivia had agreed to take over Charlotte's cooking duties. But not before warning everyone that she wasn't prepared to totally sacrifice her holiday on their behalf.

'Cooking is one thing—washing and cleaning is quite another,' she'd informed them firmly. 'So if you're expecting me to tidy up after you all, you'll have to think again. And, quite honestly,' she'd added, appealing to their better natures, 'I really don't think it's *too* much to expect you to keep your rooms in reasonable condition? Or to make up a rota for dusting and hoovering the downstairs rooms. OK?'

Everyone had been so relieved at her offer to take over the provision of meals that they'd happily agreed to the conditions she'd laid down. Although now, only two days into the holiday, there were already some cracks appearing in what had sounded a not too complicated arrangement.

With Dominic currently visiting the hospital with John, to check on Charlotte's progress, and the Rylands down in the town collecting everyone's ski-passes, it had been left to Tracy and Julian to clean the house this morning.

However, nothing much seemed to have been done, and, while Julian was nowhere to be seen, Tracy was busy painting her toenails in the large sitting room! Clearly, the beautiful redhead was giving every promise of being a total pain in the neck, Olivia told herself grimly.

In fact, the only time that Tracy seemed to come to life was when in Dominic's presence, batting her eyelashes up at the tall, darkly handsome man, and casually brushing her amazing breasts against him whenever possible. It was difficult to tell from the carefully guarded, impassive expression on Dominic's face whether he was attracted to the voluptuous redhead or not.

'That girl is poison ivy!' Sarah had complained, when she'd joined Olivia in the kitchen last night, offering to help prepare the evening meal. 'The way she's all over Dominic like a rash is utterly *disgusting*! I simply can't understand why Julian puts up with her behaviour?'

Olivia shrugged. 'Maybe he reckons that half a loaf is better than none?'

'How awful! Poor old Julian,' Sarah muttered with a frown, clearly appalled at the idea of anyone being trapped in such an unhappy relationship. 'It must be a tricky situation for Dominic!'

'I expect he can handle it!' Olivia muttered, slowly bending down to look in the oven.

'Tracy's obviously mad keen on Dominic. You must

have seen this sort of thing before. Do you think she'll manage to entice him into her bed?'

'I've no idea,' Olivia told her, suffering a slight sense of humour failure at being treated by the younger girl as an 'experienced older woman'.

She was only twenty-eight, for heaven's sake! she told herself with exasperation. Not really *all* that much older than Sarah—who clearly thought of Olivia as so long in the tooth that the idea of Dominic being attracted to such an ancient old crone had simply never occurred to her.

Olivia was still trying to come to terms with this new image of herself, as someone fast approaching middle age, when it became clear that Sarah wasn't prepared to drop the subject.

'Well? Do you reckon Tracy *will* manage to seduce Dominic?'

'Who knows?' Olivia shrugged. 'It certainly won't be for lack of trying if she doesn't,' she added grimly.

The young, newly married girl sighed, and shook her head. 'I simply don't understand men. Tracy's obviously pretty stupid, even if she has got a fabulous figure. So why would any man want to get involved with a woman who can't think about anything else but sex?'

However, when Olivia gave a wry snort of sardonic amusement, before rolling her eyes up at the ceiling, Sarah's cheeks flushed with embarrassment.

'Yes, that *was* a silly question, wasn't it?' she mumbled. 'No one's likely to refuse the offer of a free box of chocolates are they?' she said, before adding, 'Thank goodness that awful woman doesn't fancy Mark!'

There seemed no point in unnecessarily worrying Sarah by pointing out that if Tracy didn't succeed with Dominic, it was highly likely that the chalet's *femme fatale* would turn her attention to the next most attractive man in the party. However, Olivia told herself grimly, for all she knew Dominic might well fancy having a fling with Tracy—whose necklines seemed to be getting lower and more revealing with each passing day.

However, as she now busily scraped away at the potatoes, Olivia quickly decided that she really didn't want to delve into her own very complicated and tangled feelings about Dominic. It had been a shock to realise that the painful knots in her stomach every time she'd been forced to witness Tracy's blatant attempts at seduction were caused by the sharp, venomous grip of slimy green jealousy.

Far better to concentrate on the braised rump of veal in white wine, to be followed by an almond cream tart, which she was planning to produce for dinner tonight.

Olivia had just finished peeling the potatoes, and was rinsing out the bowl at the sink, before making the *pâte sucrée*—the sweet short pastry base for the almond tart—when she nearly jumped out of her skin as a pair of strong arms folded themselves about her slim waist.

'Heavens! You gave me a fright.' she gasped, surprise almost knocking the breath out of her body as she lent helplessly back against Dominic's tall figure, which was now trapping her neatly between himself and the sink. 'What on earth do you think you're doing, creeping up on me like that?'

'Shush! I've been tiptoeing around the house in an attempt to avoid Tracy,' he murmured quietly in her ear. 'Quite frankly, darling, that woman terrifies me!'

'Oh, yeah?' She gave a low, wry snort of cynical laughter. 'You didn't look all that "terrified" last night!' she said, before quickly deciding that any reference to her own fury at viewing the voluptuous redhead's brazen, outrageous behaviour might give him the wrong idea. She definitely didn't want Dominic to think that she was jealous—or cared *what* he got up to with that awful woman Tracy.

Unfortunately, he appeared to have an uncanny ability to read her mind.

'There's no need to be jealous, darling! Believe me— I wouldn't touch that woman with a bargepole!' he murmured, before lowering his head to press his lips to the soft skin at the back of her neck.

'Why on earth should I be jealous?' she retorted swiftly, shivering involuntarily at the touch of his warm mouth against her skin.

'In any case,' he went on softly, raising his chin and resting it gently on the top of her head as he stared out of the window, 'I'm not here to talk about Tracy. As you can see, it's a wonderfully bright, fresh day—and the slopes down the valley look particularly inviting, don't they?' he added, gazing out at the view in front of them.

He's right, Olivia told herself, staring out at the Christmas card scene of sparkling, crisp white snowcovered mountains, and the many pine trees with their snowladen branches heavy with glistening icicles.

Entranced by the scene in front of her, Olivia was quickly jerked back to the present as Dominic's arms tightened about her slim figure and he quickly buried his face in her hair for a moment before saying, 'Come on— let's get out of here and go skiing, hmm?'

'I can't!' she protested. 'I still haven't finished getting everything ready for dinner tonight. And then—'

'To hell with it! Everyone's *quite* capable of feeding themselves. If they're that desperate, they can go out to a local restaurant,' he told her firmly. 'Of course, if you insist on staying here in the kitchen...' he added huskily, quickly slipping his hands beneath her sweater and running them up over her silk shirt to caress her breasts '...then I'm *really* not going to be able to resist the temptation to make love to you, and...'

'OK—OK,' she gasped, trembling as he brushed his fingers over her suddenly hard, swollen nipples. 'But it'll take me a few minutes to get into my ski-clothes,' she added, quickly twisting away from the tall figure which had been pinning her so firmly to the sink.

'I don't care how long it takes you to get ready. Just as long as we can creep out of the house without alerting Tracy,' he told her in a low voice. 'You simply won't believe it,' he added with a grimace, 'but when I slipped quietly past the open doorway of the sitting room just now, the awful girl was covering her toenails with what looked like bright blue metallic paint!'

Hurriedly running up the back stairs leading from the kitchen to the long landing above, Olivia tried not to feel too guilty about abandoning her duties in the kitchen. After all, she reasoned, they wouldn't be out on the slopes for *very* long. And so there would be plenty of time for her to both enjoy herself and still be back with enough time in hand to cook dinner for everyone.

Since it was the first time that either of them had skied that year, they decided to just take it easy for this first outing, and not attempt any of the more difficult runs. Even so, it was immediately obvious to Olivia that Dominic was a really first-class skier, and pleased when he also complimented her on her own skill and ability.

'We're well-matched—don't you think?' he grinned, when they'd taken a short break to catch their breath late in the day. 'Come on! I'll race you to the bottom of the mountain,' he called out, not giving her a chance to reply as he launched himself off down the piste.

'That was wonderful!' she called out much later, as she

came to a sudden halt beside him, the force of her action causing a small cloud of snow and ice particles to blow up around her slim figure. 'Absolutely fantastic!'

'So are you!' he told her with a broad smile as he gazed down at her slim figure, clothed in a highly fashionable, deep emerald-green ski-suit, matching her sparkling eyes, her normally pale cheeks glowing from the fresh air and exercise. She looked absolutely adorable—and he couldn't resist quickly clasping her in his arms and giving her a swift kiss, before laughing as he quickly pulled them out of the way of a group of novice skiers who were lurching dangerously down the mountain towards them.

Feeling wonderfully invigorated, and having the time of her life, it wasn't until the light began to fail and Olivia glanced guiltily down at her watch that she realised just how long she'd been away from the chalet.

'I'll have to get back,' she told Dominic with a sigh of regret. 'I've been out far longer than I intended. And even if I start cooking the moment I get in, dinner won't be ready until quite late this evening.'

'Well, that's just going to be their bad luck! Because I've already made a booking for us at a wonderful seafood restaurant at Byblos de Neige. And don't even *think* of arguing with me, Olivia,' he told her in a hard, firm voice. 'I'm only out here in France because I wanted to spend time with you. So, I'm damned if I'll let you be confined to the kitchen, like Cinderella, when we could be enjoying each other's company.'

'But I can't—'

'Leave the rest of them to fend for themselves? Of course you can!' he retorted. 'It's not as though they're going to starve, is it? There are masses of really good restaurants in and around the town—at least two of which have been awarded the coveted Michelin stars for the standard of their food and cooking. So I'm certainly not going to feel sorry for the rest of the party—and neither should you!'

In the face of such strong determination to enjoy her company—had he *really* only joined the skiing party to be with her?—Olivia found herself weakly agreeing that...well...maybe the other people staying in the chalet were quite capable of looking after themselves.

'Right! Now we've settled that important point—I think the next thing is for us to find somewhere to have a nice, quiet drink before dinner, don't you?' he announced, swiftly helping her to remove her skis, balancing them casually on his shoulder alongside his own, before firmly taking hold of her hand as they trudged back to the car.

'That was wonderful,' she sighed happily, placing her knife and fork back down on the empty plate in front of her, much later that evening. 'No,' she added with a slight shake of her head, 'I really couldn't manage another mouthful. Just coffee, please.'

'It's been fun today, hasn't it?' he drawled, leaning back in his chair and smiling at the girl sitting on the other side of the table.

She nodded. 'Yes, it has. And you were quite right—there's no earthly reason why I should have got it so firmly into my head that I had to do the cooking for everyone.

Although, Olivia acknowledged silently to herself, without Dominic's strong vocal support she would probably have never summoned up enough courage to tell the other members of the chalet party to look after themselves.

'I'm taking Olivia out to dinner—so you'll all have to make your own arrangements,' he'd stated in a hard, firm voice when they'd returned to the chalet after enjoying a glass of hot mulled wine at a bar in the town. 'And *you*...' he'd added, pointing a finger at Tracy. 'You can get off your lazy backside and start pulling your weight around here. Well? What are you waiting for?' he'd demanded as the redhead had stared at him in utter astonishment, it clearly being a very long time since anyone had spoken to her so forcefully. 'There's an apron hanging behind the door of the kitchen. So I suggest you go in there, put it on, and get on with producing dinner!'

Olivia didn't know how she'd managed to keep a straight face, and the rest of the house party had seemed similarly affected as, after one, quick scared glance at the arrogant, demanding expression on Dominic's face, Tracy had swiftly scuttled from the room, her entry into the kitchen accompanied by several loud bangs—possibly the result of stainless steel saucepans being hurled angrily around the kitchen.

'I dread to think what Tracy is likely to be serving up for supper tonight!' Olivia grinned across the table at Dominic. 'Although, to be fair, I do think you were a bit hard on her.'

'Rubbish! It will do her good,' he retorted firmly. 'Besides, John is intending to drive Charlotte back to the UK tomorrow. So that's going to mean two less people to feed, anyway.'

'Oh, Lord!' she exclaimed, gazing at him in dismay. 'I'd forgotten all about poor Charlotte. How could I have been so callous and...?'

'Relax. You've been to see the poor girl at least twice in the last two days—which is more than the others have.'

'But I feel so sorry for her,' Olivia told him quietly, still feeling guilty at possibly not having done enough for

Charlotte. 'Is her ankle much worse? Is that why John is taking her back home?'

Dominic shook his dark head. 'No. It seems the surgeon out here is used to these sort of fractures, and it doesn't appear likely that there'll be a problem. As far as I can make out…' He paused while a waiter removed their empty plates, before returning to the table to replenish their wine glasses and take Dominic's order of coffee for two.

'As I was saying,' he continued, 'I think John and Charlotte both came to the conclusion that there was no point in her staying at the chalet when she's released from the hospital tomorrow. As John told me,' Dominic told her with a slight caustic edge to his voice, 'he's definitely not prepared to leave Charlotte to the tender mercies of Tracy. And someone would have to stay with the girl during the day, otherwise she'd be likely to die of boredom. Which is why,' he added, 'I imagine they decided to drive back to London. Charlotte will, after all, be far more comfortable at home with her parents.'

'Is John planning to return after the trip back home to London?'

Dominic shrugged his broad shoulders. 'I don't think he's finally made up his mind one way or another. But it's probably unlikely. I think that John may well decide to come back again at the end of March—and probably ask the Rylands to join him, as well.'

'I imagine they're old friends, since they seem to get on very well,' she said, as the waiter brought the coffee to their table.

'Yes, John and Mark were at school with each other, with me, of course. But none of us knows Julian very well—and we all think he's an idiot to put up with Tracy's nonsense.'

'Well...' Olivia murmured, avoiding his gaze as she stared down at the table, drawing patterns on the cloth with the edge of her coffee spoon. 'You must admit that she is very attractive.'

Dominic gave a brief rumble of caustic laughter. 'She may be attractive—but I'm certainly old enough to know that Tracy is also trouble with a capital T!' he said firmly. 'And that brings me to one of the things I wanted to say to you this evening.'

Olivia raised her eyes swiftly to meet his. 'About Tracy?'

'No—you idiot!' He grinned. 'I couldn't care less about that stupid woman. No...I want to talk about *us* for a moment.'

Hesitating for a moment, clearly marshalling his thoughts, Dominic leaned forward, placing his large tanned hand over her nervous fingers.

'I don't want to harp back to the past—which, as far as I'm concerned, is dead and buried,' he told her quietly. 'However, it's a fact, isn't it, that we had a very brief, torrid affair when you were only eighteen and I was not much older, certainly in terms of experience of life, at the age of twenty-three? And now, ten years later down the road, we're not only twenty-eight and thirty-three, but we've both altered and changed over the years. In fact,' he added reflectively, 'it's probably fair to say that we've not only grown up during the intervening years but have also possibly developed into two quite different people.

'That...that seems a reasonable supposition,' she agreed, trying not to be distracted by the warmth of the long fingers clasping her hand.

'Which is why I decided to risk coming out here, to the French Alps, to spend two weeks with you, Olivia,' he told her quietly. 'The fact that I find you *very* physically attractive is obviously an important factor in our relationship—especially since I can hardly keep my hands off you!' he confessed with a wry smile. 'However, simply because one lusts after a woman, it doesn't mean that...' He hesitated a moment. 'Well, let's just say that it isn't necessarily a good basis for a strong and enduring friendship. And that's what I want, Olivia,' he added firmly. 'Which is why I hope you'll agree with me that the next ten to twelve days would seem to be a perfect opportunity—while removed from our respective jobs, duties and responsibilities—to get to know each other again, far better than we do at present.'

'Yes, well...' She glanced shyly through her eyelashes up at him, before lowering her gaze to where her hand was still clasped by his strong fingers. 'That doesn't sound too unreasonable,' she agreed quietly.

However, when they returned late at night to the chalet, to discover all the lights turned off and their companions all fast asleep in their respective bedrooms, Dominic immediately made it clear that his concept 'getting to know one another again' included the night as well as the day.

'Now come on, Olivia!' he murmured as he followed her into her bedroom. 'Don't give me a hard time! Do you really want me to have a sleepless night, with a chair wedged under the door handle, in an attempt to keep the rapacious Tracy at bay?'

'You don't mean—?' She gazed at him with shocked eyes, scarcely able to believe—even in these liberated days—that the other girl would actually go so far as to invade his room.

'I certainly do!' he told her with a grin, quickly deciding to keep to himself the fact that he'd been forced to eject the voluptuous redhead from the bathroom that very morning, after she'd slipped in whilst he was shaving.

It was a very small room, and with all that amount of abundant flesh in front of him, and not much room for manoeuvre, it had been a close call!

'Ah! So now I'm supposed to save you from a fate worse than death?' Olivia murmured, trying to maintain a cool, sophisticated smile on her lips, although her legs were trembling as if made of jelly, and her heart thumping like a sledgehammer.

'Absolutely right!' he agreed, pulling her towards him, his dark head descending to take possession of her lips and effectively silencing any further protest she might make.

Olivia gave a faint, inarticulate moan as the warm touch of his mouth unleashed a wild tide of sensations which immediately obliterated all conscious thought. As happened every time she found herself in his arms, his lips and the hard strength of his body pressed so closely to her own seemed to contain the bewitching enchantment which she'd always known within his embrace.

Except that now...now that she was a mature adult, her feelings seemed deeper and more intense. And his kiss, initially a gentle caress as he savoured the sweetness of her lips, was now becoming more demanding as his tongue devoured the soft, moist inner darkness of her mouth.

Clinging helplessly to his broad shoulders, it seemed to Olivia as if she was almost melting with ecstasy beneath the touch of the hands roaming slowly and erotically over her body. Her gasps of pleasure were provoking a deep groan from his throat, and a moment later she found herself being swept up in his arms.

Striding swiftly across the bedroom, he gently lowered her down onto the bed, gazing at her in the soft lamplight with such a fiercely intent, aroused expression that she

practically melted beneath the sweeping tide of hot desire
flooding through her body.

'We're both wearing too many clothes!' he growled
impatiently. And while one part of her mind was able to
acknowledge the expertise with which this sexually experienced man deftly undid the buttons of her silk blouse,
then smoothly unzipped and slid the velvet trousers from
her long limbs, quickly followed by her brief scraps of
underwear, before stripping off his own clothes, she was
also aware of his breathing quickening at the sight of her
pale, naked body, and the way his fingers trembled as they
brushed over her flesh, his breath catching in his throat as
she raised her arms to wind them around his dark head.

'My sweet, lovely Olivia...' he groaned as she arched
her body against him, surrendering herself to the demanding possession of his lips and hands without restraint,
quivering beneath the heat of his fingers as he caressed
her soft breasts and the gentle swell of her hips. And
though it seemed as if she was helplessly trapped within
the grip of an ancient, primeval force that was almost
totally beyond her own control, feverish with a passionate
desire she'd striven so hard to deny, her body was now
pulsating with a deep hunger and need that demanded and
cried out for satisfaction.

'Olivia!' he breathed thickly, a low moan breaking
from his throat as her hands moved enticingly over his
strong body, the blood seeming to drum loudly in his head
as he felt his self-control shattering beneath the soft, intimate caress of her fingers and the driving urge of his
own powerful erection.

Locked in passion, there was no part of her that did not
respond to him, no inch of flesh that didn't quiver and
tremble beneath the electrifying effect as he sensually caressed her flesh with his mouth and hands. And, as the

ever-increasing tension became almost more than she could bear, it seemed as if they both lost all self-control, her breathless entreaties for satisfaction provoking a deep growl from his throat as he swiftly parted her thighs, his fiercely thrusting body leading her through a wild, tempestuous storm of mounting excitement until pleasure exploded within her in wave upon convulsive wave, before she felt herself floating back slowly down to earth, once more.

Afterwards, as they lay quietly entwined together, her head cradled on his arm, his face buried in the fragrant cloud of her tawny-gold hair as he whispered soft, sweetly tender endearments, Olivia knew that she had never been so happy and content. And that, whatever happened in the future, her basic love for this man, while altered and enriched from the emotion she'd felt as a young girl, was intrinsically the same as it always had been.

The next ten days and nights seemed to merge together in Olivia's mind, into a glistening and shining stream of delight and blissful happiness. It truly was, as Dominic said, a very special period, when they seemed to be discovering a completely new world of their own. One that seemed to have no boundaries as they swept down the snowcovered mountains together, enjoying the freedom and lack of all responsibilities which normally constrained their lives back home.

Skiing all day, or wandering hand in hand through the town, peering through the windows of shops and expensive boutiques—in one of which Dominic had insisted on buying her some exotic lingerie that, in terms of money for weight, could be matched only by the price of a very rare postage stamp!—Olivia found herself not only totally

MARY LYONS   141

content, but happier than she'd ever been in the whole of her life.

Their happiness in one another's company, and their absorption in each other, had not gone unnoticed amongst their companions at the chalet, of course.

The black looks and spiteful remarks from Tracy were clear evidence that she'd put two and two together to make four. But it had clearly taken Sarah some time to realise that, although Olivia might be an old lady of twenty-eight, the tall and slim blonde woman was still capable of attracting the darkly glamorous Dominic FitzCharles.

'I'm sorry...you must have thought me an absolute idiot when I made those remarks about Dominic and Tracy,' Sarah confessed one day with a shame-faced grin. 'It's just that I never thought, somehow...'

'That someone with one foot in the grave might not be entirely over the hill?' Olivia laughed.

'Oh, no! I don't mean that,' Sarah protested quickly. 'I'm absolutely *delighted* that Tracy's nose is so clearly out of joint. She does nothing but sulk all day!' The younger girl giggled.

But Olivia was far too happy to worry about Tracy— sulky or otherwise. And although she wasn't a fool, and knew very well that such happiness could only be short-lived, that she and Dominic would soon have to return to the real world, where the daily nature of work and business meetings would gradually erode their current happiness and euphoria, she would never regret having had this time with Dominic.

But, as she had always known, good things must come to an end. And, although she might have wanted to spend her last evening at Courchevel alone with him, she was quite content to fall in with Dominic's plans for everyone

in the party to attend a farewell dinner at Jacques' Bar—
one of the most welcoming and best-value restaurants in
the town—before going on to enjoy themselves at a nightclub.

Despite being blissfully happy, Olivia hadn't lost the
ability or the habit of making her own decisions. And
there had been a brief spat between herself and Dominic
when she'd discovered, earlier in the evening, that he'd
torn up her return ticket on the Eurostar, and had used his
mobile phone to arrange their transport across the English
Channel by boat.

'But really, Dominic—it will be freezing at this time
of year!' she'd protested. OK...yes, I do want to travel
back with you,' she'd finally agreed, despite not being too
pleased at his destroying her ticket without any reference
to her own wishes. 'But why go by boat? I thought you
arrived here via the Channel Tunnel?'

But when he'd pointed out that the weather was likely
to be reasonable, and that the exclusive Club Class
Lounge on the boat was comfortable, and they could enjoy
a peaceful light lunch on the way home, Olivia had merely
shrugged, realising that once Dominic had made up his
mind there was really no point in arguing with him.

In the event, the group's last meal together had been a
great success, and everyone got on really well. Even
Tracy, forgetting her sulks, clearly made an effort. And,
although Olivia hated to admit it, the luscious redhead was
looking spectacularly beautiful in a gold lurex, slightly
over the top long jersey dress, the soft material clinging
like limpet to the girl's magnificent figure.

As for the neckline...! Olivia had nearly laughed aloud
as all three men had stopped in their tracks, their eyes out
on stalks, as they viewed the low V-shaped neckline, open

almost as far as her waist and exposing almost all of her magnificent breasts!

'Whatever you do, Tracy, don't turn around too quickly in that dress—or we'll all be arrested!' Dominic laughed. And for once Tracy seemed reasonably human, merely giggling in response to his remark before slipping her arm through the bemused figure of Julian and giving him a brief peck on the cheek.

Maybe those two have made up? Olivia thought, and although it didn't seem likely, she hoped for Julian's sake that they had.

Sarah hadn't been able to take the same relaxed attitude towards her husband's difficulty in tearing his eyes away from so much luscious flesh.

'That dress of Tracy's is absolutely *disgusting*!' she declared through tight lips, when she and Olivia adjourned to the ladies' cloakroom at the end of the meal before going on to the nightclub.

'Oh, come on, Sarah!' Olivia grinned at the younger girl. 'Let's face it, Tracy really *has* got a fantastic figure.'

'Yes, I know,' Sarah muttered gloomily. 'That's what I'm complaining about!'

Olivia laughed. 'Relax! If I know Tracy, I'll bet you anything you like that she's planning to dump Julian at the nightclub and find herself a more glamorous and much richer man! And, from the way she's looking tonight,' Olivia added cynically, 'I imagine she's likely to be highly successful, don't you?'

'You're probably right.' Sarah nodded. 'Actually, I don't care *what* she does—just as long as she keeps her hooks out of my dear husband!'

After arriving at the nightclub, and making their way to the table which had been reserved for them by Dominic, it seemed as though Olivia's forecast had been correct. Because Tracy immediately attracted the obvious admiration and attention of several men from the nearby tables.

Gazing around at her surroundings, it seemed to Olivia that the nightclub was full of well-known faces to which she couldn't quite put a name. Although she did spot one well-known film star and his wife, attracting the attention of the paparazzi, who appeared to be able to snap away without fear of being thrown out by the management.

Quite astonishingly, the bottles of champagne ordered by Dominic seemed to have at last loosened Julian's vocal cords. Having spent most of the holiday virtually monosyllabic, he had suddenly launched into telling one amusing story after another. And, since he was very funny, he soon had the whole table in stitches of laughter. Only Tracy, closely entwined on the dance floor with a dashing-looking Frenchman, wasn't appreciative of her boyfriend's emergence into the limelight.

'Maybe we've underestimated Julian,' she murmured to Dominic, who, unlike the rest of the table, was confining himself to drinking cans of sparkling tonic water. When she had raised an eyebrow at this, he'd explained that someone had to remain sober, to drive the party back to the chalet—a responsible attitude which she found quite impressive under the circumstances.

The evening wore on. Dominic and Olivia had just returned from the dance floor, and were pouring themselves a drink, when she noticed that Tracy—who'd found herself swiftly abandoned, when the dashing Frenchman's slim and attractive wife had called him to heel—was glowering at her across the table. Clearly the other girl resented the fact that she and Dominic were so clearly happy and absorbed with one another.

Whether it was the result of too much alcohol, or

whether Tracy was motivated by some darker, deeper resentment at having been frustrated in her attempt to seduce Dominic, something clearly snapped in the red-headed girl's brain.

'Well, Dominic, darling!' she drawled loudly, before tossing a glass of champagne down her throat. 'You've obviously had a *really* good holiday! But it's not going to be so much fun for Olivia, is it? Not when she gets home and discovers that you're going to dump her—like all your other glamorous girlfriends. Sorry, sweetie!' she added, turning to give a false, beaming smile at Olivia. 'I hope you haven't made the *big* mistake of thinking he's going to ask you to marry him?'

Quite what Tracy had expected to achieve by her catty remarks, perhaps even she didn't know. However, in the appalled, deathly silence which followed her words, Dominic immediately leapt to his feet.

'I'm delighted to tell you that Tracy is utterly wrong!' he announced, before turning to smile down at the startled face of the girl sitting next to him.

Swiftly bending down and scooping up something from the table, he quickly grabbed hold of Olivia's left hand. 'It's not the traditional diamond, of course,' he grinned, slipping a ring-pull from a soft drink can onto the third finger of her left hand. 'However, as far as *I'm* concerned, I definitely intend to marry Olivia. So, I think you can all regard this as our engagement party!'

There was another moment's stunned silence, with everyone around the table staring openmouthed in astonishment as Dominic, pulling Olivia's trembling and dazed figure to her feet, placed his arms swiftly around her before claiming her lips in a long, warm and tender kiss.

And then everyone was laughing and clapping and wishing the couple much happiness, the noise at their table attracting not only smiles and congratulations from the people on the nearby tables, but also the attention of the paparazzi.

Shocked and speechless by the speed of what had happened, and yet realising that she mustn't be stupid enough to take this mad 'proposal' seriously, Olivia laughed up at Dominic's handsome face, blinking in the light of the photographer's flashbulbs as she joked, 'No one's ever asked me to marry them with the ring from a can of tonic before!'

'We'll go shopping in Bond Street for a better version just as soon as we get home!' he promised her with a wide grin.

She laughed and shook her head. 'I should live so long!' she grinned.

'My God—I hope so!' he laughed, before folding her tightly in his arms once more.

CHAPTER EIGHT

'DON'T be ridiculous! We both know that it was only a joke. *Of course* we're not engaged to be married!' Olivia told Dominic firmly as he drove them away from the chalet the next morning.

She continued to repeat the words like a mantra—despite suffering from a mammoth hangover from last night's party—as he drove through Moutiers and Albertville. However, as they approached Lyon, Dominic finally lost his temper.

'For goodness sake, shut up—darling!' he growled, his words resulting, as far as he was concerned, in a sulky if blessedly silent 'fiancée'.

'What you need, my dearest Olivia, is a long hot bath followed by a glass of champagne and a really excellent dinner,' he said, as they finally reached the southeast suburbs of Reims.

'Oh, no!' she moaned, shuddering at the thought of imbibing any more alcohol.

Dominic laughed as he drove the Range Rover through massive wrought-iron gates towards an elegant cream-coloured château in a park-like setting of sweeping lawns and mature trees.

'Nevertheless, I can assure you that you'll feel a great deal better after a reviving glass of sparkling champagne. And this is, of course, the perfect place to drink it,' he added, coming to a halt outside the imposing entrance to the château. 'Since we are, after all, in the very heart of the Champagne area.'

It had to be quite the grandest hotel she'd ever stayed in, Olivia told herself later as, following Dominic's orders, she lay in an enormous bathtub, relishing the wonderfully hot water liberally sprinkled with aromatic oils.

From the moment they'd entered the imposing foyer of pale beige marble, whose walls were hung with old tapestries, before being led to their palatial suite with its huge windows overlooking the park, Olivia had definitely begun to feel slightly overawed. She couldn't remember having ever stayed in a hotel suite with *two* bathrooms, for heaven's sakes!

Her thoughts were interrupted as Dominic strolled into the bathroom, carrying a glass of champagne in each hand, his tall figure wrapped in one of the hotel's white terry towelling gowns.

'And now for your medicine,' he said, before giving a low rumble of laughter as she quickly slipped down beneath the surface of the water, liberally covered in white foamy bubbles, leaving only her head visible.

'Really, darling! It seems a bit late in the day to try and hide that lovely figure of yours.' He grinned at the faint flush rising up over her pale cheeks. 'Over the past few days—and nights—I have, if you recall, had many opportunities of seeing your delicious naked body.'

'Yes, well...' she murmured, blushing again as she lifted a soapy hand to receive the glass he was handing her. 'It seems a bit strange, prancing nude around this extraordinarily luxurious suite. I hope to goodness you can afford it?'

'Well, if I can't we can always offer to do the washing up after dinner,' he told her, pulling up a stool and sitting down beside the bath before ordering her to drink up.

Olivia glared at him. 'Don't bully me!' she protested. However, as so often seemed to be the case, Dominic proved to be maddeningly right, she told herself as she sipped the cool sparkling liquid. 'By the way, I hope you were joking about not having enough money to pay the bill? Because, although I've got one or two credit cards on me, they may not be accepted by this hotel.'

Dominic grinned at her. 'Yes, darling—I *was* just joking about not being able to pay the bill.' He smiled lazily down at her for a few moments. 'I find it rather refreshing to realise that you must be one of the very few women of my acquaintance who clearly doesn't realise that I'm a *very* wealthy man. Which is nothing but a pure accident of birth, of course, as you know,' he added quickly. 'And, when all is said and done, not *that* important as far as human relationships are concerned.'

Olivia shrugged. 'Quite honestly, what with one thing and another, I haven't really given the state of your finances any thought. I mean, we've had other...er...'

'Other things to think about?' He grinned at her. 'Quite right, so we have. However, I just wanted you to know that I'm quite capable of supporting a wife—and any number of children, for that matter—in a state of reasonable comfort.'

'Oh, Dominic, you know very well that our so-called "engagement" was just one of those things that happen sometimes at the end of a rather drunken evening,' she told him. 'And, yes, it *was* a good joke. But we're now having to return to the real world, right? Where you're a very busy man and I've got a business to run.

'And although I'm not too proud to admit that the last couple of weeks have been, without a shadow of doubt, the most wonderful of my life I'm not a fool,' she told him sadly. 'It really *was* a very special, precious time out of mind. And I will always look back on our holiday in

Courchevel as being a period of great joy and happiness. But you must see that it's now over.'

'I don't see anything of the sort,' he told her dismissively. 'As far as I'm concerned we're engaged; we are going to get married—and that is that!'

'Oh, come on, Dominic! You're just not thinking straight,' she pointed out grimly. 'What about your mother?'

'What about her?' He frowned.

Olivia gave an unhappy snort of laughter. 'Not only is she the most *terrifying* woman that I've ever met, but she's hardly likely to welcome *me* with open arms, is she?'

However, after arrogantly stating that he was master in his own house, and could do exactly what he pleased, Dominic adamantly refused to discuss the matter any further.

Claiming that he was starving, he swept her off downstairs to the dining room, banning all discussion of their future during the wonderful meal that followed. And when they returned to their bedroom suite he gave her no opportunity to protest any further as he swiftly and, alas, so easily demonstrated the power of his attraction for her— seemingly able, in the twinkling of an eye, to turn the protesting body in his arms into that of a pliant, willing slave, only conscious of the need to respond to his erotic, sensual touch and ardently welcoming his vigorous possession.

You're nothing but a weak, feeble woman! Olivia told herself the next morning as she slipped into a pair of comfortable dark blue trousers, cream polo neck sweater and warm navy blue blazer, ready for the remainder of their journey back to London. And really there was little point in continuing to point out the impossibility of their marriage. Because once they'd both returned to their normal lives in England Dominic would be finally able to see, as clearly as she did, that it simply wouldn't work.

It had taken her a long time, of course, but she could now acknowledge the fact that, despite all that had happened, she had never stopped loving the man she'd first met when she was barely eighteen. Unfortunately that wasn't enough, she thought sadly, walking over the soft carpet to stare out of the tall, floor-to-ceiling windows overlooking the park outside the hotel.

Because she really *wasn't* a fool. Whatever one's view of the aristocracy, Dominic's title and large estate, including a wonderful old castle which was open daily to the public in the summer, did carry with it considerable responsibilities.

Far from being a playboy, he took his duties as a magistrate and his chairmanship of various local charities very seriously indeed. Not to mention the fact that running a large estate of some ten thousand acres was virtually a full-time job in itself. And it naturally followed that his wife, whoever she might be, would be expected to support and aid him in all his endeavours.

However, Olivia found it almost impossible to imagine herself in the role of Dominic's wife. Even in this day and age of equality, when many wives of prominent men maintained their own careers, she was certain that Dominic would automatically expect—if not insist—that she give up her business, sell her house in London and take up residence in Charlbury Castle as the current Countess of Tenterden.

It was a daunting prospect. And not one to be undertaken lightly. Indeed, she found it virtually impossible to imagine herself opening a local flower show, for instance, let alone having to run and manage a huge old castle. And then there was the problem of having to cope with his mother.

Dominic had been, of course, totally dismissive over the possibility of a difficult situation between the two women. But Olivia foresaw enormous problems in having to deal with the tough, arrogant old woman, who was hardly likely to want to let go of the reins which she'd been handling for so long. And the prospect of living in a house—however large it might be—over which she had no control could only lead to great unhappiness.

Still…she consoled herself, as Dominic finished packing his suitcase and they went downstairs to breakfast, it was only the members of the chalet party and a few unknown strangers who'd witnessed his dramatic, if slightly mad proposal of marriage. And, even if Mark, Sarah and the others *did* gossip about what had happened, it was highly unlikely that anyone else would believe such a crazy story. And even Dominic himself might well come to regret such a foolish impulse, and be grateful to her for not having taken him too seriously.

These comforting thoughts sustained Olivia as far as Calais. But, on boarding the boat and entering the privacy of the club class lounge, where champagne, coffee and the Sunday papers awaited them, she found herself suddenly thrown into a state of almost terminal shock.

Together with the simultaneous roar of laughter from Dominic, and deep, utterly horrified groans from herself, she realised that not only their friends at the chalet but now also the whole wide world would be aware of his unconventional proposal!

'I don't believe it!' she moaned, staring down glassy-eyed at the full page, in a tabloid Sunday newspaper, containing various pictures of Dominic putting the can 'ring' on her finger.

'That's rather a good picture of you,' he drawled, leaning over her shoulder as he pointed to one of the photographs showing Olivia's head tilted back as she laughed up into his handsome face.

'Although I'm not sure I go for the cheeky headline: "EARL RING-PULLS HIS BIRD!"—the rest of it isn't too bad,' Dominic told her with a grin.

'In fact, I'm rather flattered by that bit about "the suave, sophisticated Earl of Tenterden"!' He laughed. 'It's a lot better than the rather sedate description in my paper,' he added, placing his copy of the *Sunday Times*, open at the relevant page, on the table in front of her.

'Oh, *no*!' she moaned, quickly burying her face in her hands, but not before she'd had one brief, appalled glimpse of the headline: 'WEDDING ORGANISER ARRANGES HER OWN MARRIAGE!'

'But how did these pictures get into the papers? And so quickly?' she muttered tearfully, utterly shocked and feeling quite sick at the sight of herself plastered all over the newsprint.

'The paparazzi, I presume,' Dominic told her with a shrug. 'If you remember, a number of them, plus some reporters, were milling around the nightclub. They were, of course, chiefly interested in getting a few unguarded photos of both that French film star and his wife, and that Greek shipping heiress who's always bolting from one husband to another.

'So...' He gave another shrug. 'It looks as though we were just unlucky to be caught by them. On the other hand,' he added, 'maybe it isn't such a bad idea. It will certainly save us the trouble of having to tell our friends that we're getting married, won't it?'

He grinned at Olivia's heartfelt low groan, as she sat

slumped over the table, her head buried in her folded arms.

It had been a complete accident that the paparazzi had been present in the nightclub, of course. But really, Dominic told himself, struggling not to laugh out loud, they had done him a considerable favour. His darling Olivia, who'd been trying very hard to wriggle off the hook, would now find it extremely difficult to escape the net closing in on her. All the same...it might be just as well to keep up the pressure.

'I'm just going out on deck for a breath of fresh air,' he told the huddled figure sitting beside him, his mouth twitching with amusement as she merely gave another deep, low groan.

Giving her a comforting hug and a pat on the shoulder, he rose and walked across the floor of the lounge, taking out his mobile phone and punching in Directory Enquiries.

'Yes, I'd like the telephone numbers of *The Times* and the *Daily Telegraph*, please,' he murmured, closing the door of the lounge firmly behind him.

'Oh, Olivia! I'm just so *thrilled*!' Mo exclaimed, clearly so anxious to greet her employer that she'd rushed into the office while still in the middle of removing her coat. 'First of all there were all those wonderful pictures in the paper yesterday. And now the official announcement! Did Lord Tenterden *really* ask you to marry him by putting a ring-pull from one of those soft drink cans over your finger? *How romantic!*'

'Please, Mo—don't you start!' Olivia moaned, feeling like death warmed up after a sleepless night, tossing and turning in her bed as she tried to think what on earth she was going to do. 'It was just a silly joke—that's all.'

Mo stared at her in utter bewilderment. 'But…but what about the announcement in the papers today?'

'What announcement? What papers?' Olivia muttered, taking another sip from the cup of black coffee on the desk in front of her as she tried to get a firmer grip on life.

'Well, I haven't seen the *Daily Telegraph*—but the announcement of your engagement is definitely here, in *The Times*,' Mo told her, quickly opening the paper and folding it back, before placing it on the desk in front of Olivia.

'There you are,' she said, jabbing a finger down on the newsprint. 'It couldn't be much plainer, could it?'

Mo was quite right—it couldn't.

Because there, in fiery letters that seemed to leap from the newspaper, she read:

FORTHCOMING MARRIAGES
The Earl of Tenterden
and the Hon O. R. Johnson
The engagement is announced between the Earl of Tenterden, of Charlbury Castle, Kent, and Olivia Rose, only daughter of Lord Bibury, of Lidgate Manor, Kent, and the late Lady Bibury.

'But I don't understand… I certainly never sent an announcement to the papers!' Olivia wailed. 'Who on earth could have done such a thing?'

And then, as her cry echoed around the office, she knew exactly *who* had placed the announcement in the paper.

'I'll kill him!' she ground out through clenched teeth, springing up from her chair and pacing up and down the small office in front of the astonished figure of Mo, who was gazing at her employer as if she'd taken leave of her senses.

'That lousy...rotten...double-dealing rat!' she yelled, swearing violently under her breath before picking up a small ornament from the top of the filing cabinet beside her and hurling it violently against the wall. 'I know what he's up to! It's all a deliberate ploy—just to make sure that I'm going to sign on the dotted line. Well, I *won't* be bullied like this!'

'Olivia...*Olivia*!' Mo called out. 'For heaven's sake—calm down and explain what's wrong.'

As Mo's voice finally managed to pierce the red cloud of dense anger in her head, Olivia struggled to try and bring her overwhelming flash of bad temper under some sort of control.

'Yes...yes, I'm sorry,' she mumbled, before giving an exhausted sigh of deep depression and walking slowly back to sit down behind her desk. 'I'm sorry. I just can't quite cope with anything this morning,' she mumbled, leaning back in her chair and closing her eyes for a moment.

Mo hesitated, staring down at the exhausted girl before giving a slight shake of her head and leaving the room, returning a few minutes later with a glass of water and some aspirins.

'Here, I think you'd better take these,' she said quietly, pulling up a chair and sitting down across the desk from Olivia. 'Now, why don't you tell me all about it?'

Olivia gave a heavy sigh. 'It's so complicated. I can't even think where to start,' she muttered, before smiling gratefully at the older woman as she swallowed the pills.

'How about starting at the beginning and going on to the end?' Mo told her with a slight smile.

But, after Olivia had given a shrug and related all that had happened during the two weeks she'd been away, she found herself startled by her assistant's reaction to the story.

'Well, at least there's one thing that's as plain as the nose on my face,' Mo told her with a grin. '*You* may be full of doubts and uncertainties—but his lordship certainly seems to know his own mind!'

'No, he doesn't.' Olivia shook her head. 'I keep telling you—it was just a joke. A sort of silly, rather juvenile gesture, actually. The sort of thing one does as a teenager at the end of an evening. I mean, it's not the *normal* way to propose marriage, is it?' she added grumpily. 'At my age, I don't think it's too unreasonable to expect something a lot more sophisticated than *that*!'

Mo regarded her silently for a few moments. 'Do you love him?' she said at last.

'That's got nothing to do with it,' Olivia muttered, not quite meeting the older woman's eyes. 'I just don't like being railroaded, and…'

'I'd say that it has *everything* to do with it,' Mo told her bluntly. 'If you're definitely *not* in love with the man, then the answer's very simple. All I have to do—and I can easily take care of it this morning—is send a notice to both *The Times* and the *Telegraph*, regretting to announce that your marriage to the Earl of Tenterden will not take place. We've had to do it before, for clients who've broken off their engagements, haven't we?'

Olivia sighed. 'Yes, I suppose we have.'

Watching as conflicting expressions flickered back and forth across her employer's face, Mo eventually said, 'Well, do you want me to send the papers a notice cancelling your engagement?'

Olivia gave another heavy sigh. 'No…yes…I don't know,' she muttered helplessly.

'Ah! So you *are* in love with him?'

'Yes, damn it!' Olivia sighed with exasperation. 'Yes, of course I'm in love with the rotten man! But I don't like being railroaded like this, and I deeply resent having stupid pictures and even worse comments splashed all over the newspapers. And I still don't understand *why*, after a wonderfully happy two weeks, he had to do something so stupid with that ring from a can of tonic water. It doesn't make sense!'

'Oh, I don't know,' the older woman mused quietly. 'If, as you say, you'd both had this wonderful time together, well away from the pressures of everyday life, he may well have feared that once you returned back home you'd get caught up in what is, after all, a fairly hectic business.'

'But that's the whole point, you see,' Olivia told her earnestly. 'I'm not a fool. I could see that, although we had a wonderful time, we were both going to have to return to the real world. Which is precisely *why* I've been refusing, ever since that mad gesture of his, to take him seriously.'

Mo regarded her silently for a moment. 'I'm slightly puzzled as to why it hasn't occurred to you that the Earl might be quite capable of coming to the same conclusion,' she said at last. 'I take it the man isn't a fool? That he's perfectly capable of realising that you'd both have little time, or opportunity, to recapture the happiness which you'd known together on holiday? So,' she added as Olivia remained silent, 'maybe he just decided to strike while the iron was hot? To make sure of you while he could? And really, you know, it *was* a very romantic gesture. I wish somebody had proposed to me like that,' she added with a heavy sigh.

'Yes...yes, I can see that you've got a point,' Olivia muttered, before the telephone on the desk started ringing.

'Take that call, can you?' she added, waving a distracted hand at the instrument. 'I really don't think I can cope with anyone just at the moment.'

Unfortunately, that was the first of what seemed an unending stream of phone calls from Olivia's friends and past clients, all of whom had either seen the photographs in the Sunday papers or read of her engagement today.

Without exception, they seemed to be absolutely delighted, and, rather touchingly, their good wishes and congratulations concerned their delight that she'd found true love and personal happiness with the man of her dreams—rather than complimenting her on having captured one of the most eligible bachelors in Britain.

Although Hugo, of course, teased her unmercifully when, finding her telephone virtually engaged non-stop, he turned up at lunchtime with a bottle of champagne in his hand.

'Who's a clever girl, then!' he joked, before insisting that Mo produce three glasses, so that they could toast his sister's future life and happiness. 'But I can't really see you as a countess somehow, Livvy.' He grinned. 'Although, given time, I expect you'll turn into a dreadful old trout—just like Dominic's mother!'

'Don't you start!' she groaned. 'I've been telling Mo all morning that it's just a joke which seems to have got completely out of control. In fact,' she added with a weary shrug, 'I'm expecting Dominic to ring me any moment—with his tail firmly between his legs!—confessing that he's made a great mistake and humbly begging my pardon. And he'd *better* apologise properly—because I'm just about ready to wring the swine's neck!'

'Oh, don't be such an idiot, Livvy,' her brother told her, handing her a glass of champagne. 'Even I could see he was crazy about you. So why you seem to think that he's playing some sort of joke, I really don't—'

'Just a minute!' she exclaimed, her figure suddenly stiffening as she turned to stare fixedly at him. 'Exactly *when* did you "see" that Dominic was supposedly crazy about me? I didn't know that you'd met him lately. Maybe you'd like to tell me about it?' she added in an ominously quiet voice.

Her brother shrugged his shoulders. 'Really, Livvy, I can't possibly be expected to remember that sort of thing. It's really not important, and...'

'*Hugo!* I've known you all my life—so don't try and prevaricate with *me!*' she ground out. 'Exactly *when* did you meet Dominic?'

'Oh, well, if you must know, he looked me up about a month ago,' her brother admitted sheepishly.

'And?'

'Now, Livvy, calm down!' he told her hurriedly, as Mo, quickly deciding to return to the peace and quiet of her own office, tiptoed from the room. 'I can promise you, the reason why he got in touch with me had absolutely *nothing* to do with you. In fact, he hardly even mentioned your name—only very briefly, at the end of our conversation.'

Olivia gazed at him sternly for a moment. 'So why didn't you tell me that you'd met him? And exactly *why* did he contact you?' she added suspiciously.

Her brother gave a heavy sigh. 'I probably should have told you about meeting up with Dominic—but when he asked me not to, because it might be slightly awkward, I agreed not to say anything.'

'Ah-ha!' Olivia glared at him, before taking a deep breath. 'OK. We're going to get to the bottom of this—

right now!' she declared. 'So sit down, Hugo, and tell me exactly what you've been up to!'

Ten minutes later she leaned back in the chair behind her desk.

'Well, Dominic certainly seems to have been very busy involving our family in his nefarious schemes, doesn't he?' she told her brother bitterly, having listened with increasing incredulity to how Hugo had been approached by a firm of city lawyers. They, apparently, were acting for an unknown client who was in the process of building a brand new, modern-day version of an English village on some land on the client's estate. It had only been when he'd been awarded the contract that Hugo had met Dominic—who had turned out to be the landowner in question—to finalise details of the designs which Hugo had submitted.

'I won that contract fair and square,' Hugo was now telling her firmly. 'You may not believe me—but I've seen some of the other designs which were submitted. And I've got *no* problem in believing that my suggestions were far and away better than any of the others. In fact,' he added, 'it was precisely *because* Dominic feared that it might look like some kind of personal favour to an old friend that he asked me not to tell anyone. And, since we hadn't met for goodness knows how many years, I was happy to respect his wishes.'

'Humph!' Olivia muttered. It all sounded very reasonable. But she was quite certain that she smelt a rat somewhere in the story. Unfortunately, she just couldn't quite put her finger on it at the moment.

'Just a minute,' she said quickly. 'How did Dominic track you down? You've only been living in that small flat of yours for a few months.'

Hugo shrugged. 'I haven't a clue,' he admitted. 'However, I can faithfully promise you, Livvy, that the only time your name entered the conversation that I had with Dominic concerned the date I was due to start work. Because although I realised that I'd be an idiot not to accept such a prestigious commission, I had to tell him that the timing was lousy. I mean, we were all set to go off on holiday together, weren't we?'

'So...?'

'So Dominic was very sympathetic about the fact that he had to insist on me getting on with the job straight away. He was sure that you'd still manage to have a good holiday, and that John Graham would easily find someone else to take my place.'

Olivia stared at him in silence for a moment, before giving an exclamation of disgust. 'Oh, yes—he certainly *did* find someone to take your place. *Himself!* Talk about a clever, double-crossing, conniving rat!'

'Oh, come on! You're becoming totally paranoiac,' her brother told her grimly. 'For heaven's sake, Livvy, we're talking about a multi-million pound development—right? Now, I don't care how much he loves you. There's no way any man with an ounce of sense would take the risk of jeopardising his investment by employing his girl-friend's brother just so he could have a few days' holiday with the love of his life. It simply doesn't make sense. Surely you must see that?'

Olivia gave a heavy sigh. 'Yes, I suppose you're right,' she admitted slowly, forced to realise that Dominic was, first and foremost, a businessman. 'It just all seems so weird, that's all. And, really, you know, I've *never* come across so many "coincidences" in all my life as I have over the last month. Maybe I'm going senile, like Dad?'

'Don't be an idiot!' her brother laughed. 'Incidentally, talking of Dad—have you told him your news?'

'Oh, Lord! No, I haven't,' she muttered, suddenly feeling guilty at having forgotten all about her father amidst the highly disturbing elements of her socalled engagement to Dominic. 'I meant to ring the housekeeper today, in any case, since I haven't been in touch since just before leaving for France,' she said, picking up the phone and quickly dialling a number.

'Well...I don't know,' she muttered bemusedly, replacing the receiver some minutes later. 'It *did* occur to me to wonder why, since he's clearly been so very busy, I haven't heard from my so-called "fiancé" this morning.

'However,' she told her brother, 'I'm sure you'll be as interested as I was to hear that apparently Dominic called in to see Dad this morning and now, according to Mrs Douglas, our dear father seems to have brightened up no end. And is, apparently, calling for a glass of champagne to toast—and I quote—"the happy couple"!'

'Good heavens!' Hugo exclaimed. 'I thought Dad had completely lost his marbles by now.'

'That's not a very nice expression.' Olivia frowned. 'But I must admit that he hasn't been too lucid lately. Still, maybe you can tell me what on earth Dominic was doing, calling in to see Dad, when I'm quite certain that he hasn't been anywhere near the house for the past ten years.'

'Search me!' Hugo shrugged. 'Maybe he was there to ask for permission to marry you?' he teased. 'Although it doesn't sound very likely, does it?'

By the time she'd packed Mo off home, at the end of what seemed to have been a very long day, Olivia's mind was still full of many unanswered questions. The foremost of which concerned why she'd heard nothing from Dominic today.

The whole idea of their engagement was, as she'd

maintained ever since that crazy episode in the nightclub, a total nonsense. Still, having almost deliberately caused such a furore both in France and through the medium of the press, the swine might have made an effort to contact his new 'fiancée', she told herself grumpily as she tidied up her small kitchen, hesitating for a moment before putting the remains of Hugo's bottle of champagne in the fridge.

Some celebration! she told herself grimly, leaning against the worktop for a moment while she tried to work out which, of her many gripes against Dominic, she found the most exasperating, eventually coming to the conclusion that it was her overriding feelings of impotence and frustration at not being any longer in control of her life which she minded most of all.

Just wait till I see him, she was promising herself savagely, when she heard a sharp ring on the doorbell.

'Ah-ha!' she exclaimed grimly as she opened the door to see Dominic standing on the doorstep. 'Well! If it isn't my beloved fiancé!' she added in a sarcastic drawl as she stood back to let him into the small hall. 'You seem to have been *very* busy today!'

'Tell me about it!' he muttered, his tall figure seeming to dominate the small space.

'Yes, well, that's actually *my* line,' she told him grimly over her shoulder, leading the way up the stairs and into her small sitting room. 'You've *definitely* got some explaining to do—and the list of items I want to discuss seems to be getting longer every minute. Starting with—'

'Hold it!' He held up his hand. 'I don't want to be difficult, Olivia—'

'That makes a change!' She glared at him.

'But I haven't had anything to eat since early this morning. So, if I faithfully promise to answer each and every one of your questions—utterly truthfully and to the very best of my ability—can you *please* hurry up and get changed so I can take you out to dinner? Believe me, darling, I'm famished!'

She regarded him steadily for a moment, before giving a heavy sigh. 'You're absolutely impossible, Dominic,' she told him ruefully. 'But, OK. If you really and truly *are* going to come clean with me at last?'

'Yes, you have my word of honour that I will,' he told her, before pulling her quickly into his arms and giving her a swift kiss. 'Now for God's sake hurry up—I really am starving!'

'I've never known anyone who didn't seem to function properly unless he had three square meals a day!' Olivia told him some time later as they sat on a red plush banquette at Chez Moi—one of the most romantic small restaurants in London.

'Oh, come on!' he laughed. 'Surely you realise that's the only reason I want to marry you—just so I can be sure of eating wonderful food to the end of my days?'

'The *only* reason?' she queried. 'Is that really what this has all been about, Dominic? Because, if so, you seem to have gone to a *great* deal of trouble to make sure you never go hungry! Wouldn't employing a first-class chef be slightly easier?' she added sarcastically.

He smiled lazily down at her. 'You're quite right; it most certainly would,' he agreed, taking hold of one of her hands, and lifting it to his lips. 'But you've always known in your heart of hearts, my dearest, that it's *you* I want. And, although you've given vent to a considerable amount of sound and fury, I don't believe that you've ever really doubted my intentions. Hmm?'

'Well...perhaps not,' she admitted slowly, not quite

able to meet his gaze as he stared so intently at her. 'But I'm not the sort of person who's good at coping with the unexpected. And you must admit you've given me a *very* hard time!' she added with a sudden flash of irritation as she tried to withdraw her hand from his.

'Oh, no, you don't,' he murmured, still keeping a firm grip on her fingers and quickly raising her hand to his lips once more, before turning to beckon to one of the waiters passing by the entrance to the small, semi-private dining alcove at the back of the restaurant.

'First things first,' he told her firmly, as the waiter reappeared with a silver salver on which lay a small black leather box. 'I'll discuss anything you like and answer any questions you may have—but I really do think it's time that I offered you a replacement for that aluminium ring, don't you?' he murmured, taking the box from the salver and placing it on the table in front of her.

'I have to say,' he continued as he opened the box and presented its contents to her, 'that I have a selection of at least four other rings in the restaurant's safe. However, I think this is my favourite, principally because it matches your wonderfully large green eyes,' he said, taking a huge diamond and emerald ring out of the box and sliding it over the third finger of her left hand.

'Oh, Dominic!' she gasped, staring bemusedly down at the fantastically beautiful stones glinting and sparkling in the candlelight.

'Do you like it?' he murmured.

'I love it!' she breathed, tearing her eyes away from the ring to gaze at him with starry eyes. 'And I love *you*—but...but are you *really* sure that you want to marry me?'

'With all my heart,' he told her softly, before gathering her trembling figure into his warm embrace and possessing her lips in a kiss of total commitment.

CHAPTER NINE

STARING blindly out of the window at the torrential rain pounding down out of the grey sky, Olivia gave a heavy sigh. It seemed to have been raining continuously for the past four days, ever since she'd been awoken by that telephone call from Mrs Douglas, the housekeeper at her old family home, Lidgate Manor, with the shocking news of her father's sudden death.

'Poor man, he'd seemed so much brighter lately,' the housekeeper had told her on the phone that morning. 'Really excited about your engagement, he was,' she'd added with a slight sob. 'But, dearie, it may be for the best. That's how we'd all like to go, isn't it? Quietly in our sleep.'

Mrs Douglas had, of course, been quite right. Having immediately rushed down from London, Olivia had found it extraordinarily comforting, when finally screwing up enough courage to view her father, that all trace of age and unhappiness seemed to have been wiped from his face, and that he was looking peaceful and at rest after what had been, in many ways, a deeply unhappy life.

However, as she'd rapidly learned, those left behind in this life rarely had the opportunity to grieve for the passing of their loved ones. So much of their time had to be spent dealing with the official forms. And then there were the arrangements which needed to be made concerning such distressing items as organising the funeral and burial service, dealing with lawyers, and, almost worst of all, having to reply to the many letters of condolence which seemed to arrive by every post.

'I'm sorry not to be more of a help,' Hugo had told her, on paying a brief visit to the old family home yesterday. 'But we're working flat out at the moment, and it's virtually impossible for me to take too much time away, even if I wanted to,' he'd told her with a worried frown, brushing a hand distractedly through his hair.

'It's OK. Just as long as you make sure that you're here for the funeral,' she'd told him quietly. 'Otherwise, I expect I can see to most things on my own.'

'It's so weird,' her brother had said later, walking through the house and idly running his fingers over the few remaining pieces of furniture which hadn't been sold. 'It seems so strange to find myself being addressed as Lord Bibury. I keep turning around, expecting to see Dad standing behind me. After having been plain Hugo Johnson all these years, it's just...' He'd shrugged. 'Well, I can't get used to it, that's all.'

'You will—in time,' she'd told him gently, placing a comforting hand on his shoulder for a moment, before asking whether he had any favourite hymns he'd like at the funeral in a few days' time.

In many ways, although she half resented having to make all the arrangements, and the fact that her days seemed filled with the necessity to make one decision after another, it did have the advantage of preventing her from thinking too much about her engagement. An engagement which, just at the moment, seemed to be frozen in a state of suspended animation, with nothing properly resolved between herself and Dominic.

When he'd taken her out to such a romantic dinner last week at Chez Moi, and presented her with such a magnificent engagement ring, Olivia had been confidently expecting that all her doubts and uncertainties would be resolved. Especially as Dominic had promised that he would finally explain and answer so many of the questions which had been troubling her.

And it had seemed, initially, that he would be able to keep his word.

'You know I love you,' she'd told him with a beaming smile, as plates of smoked salmon had been placed in front of them. 'But I really do think that it's time you explained *exactly* what's been going on, don't you?'

'It's difficult to know where to start.' He shrugged.

She grinned. 'As my assistant, Mo, would say: why don't you start at the beginning and go on to the end?'

'Very sensible!' he agreed with a soft laugh. 'All the same, I'm not sure, at this point in our relationship, that I particularly want to dwell on our first romance all those years ago. I'm not saying it wasn't important—because of course it was. But so much has happened to us in the intervening years that it now seems a lifetime away, doesn't it?'

She nodded. 'Yes, you're quite right; it does.'

'However, I think it's important to bear in mind that, while our earlier romance was clearly a juvenile affair for both of us, nevertheless, part of you must have remained tucked away in the corner of my mind and my heart,' he told her with a warm smile.

'And though I've obviously been involved with many other women—and I'm not going to pretend that I haven't—no one has ever seemed...' He hesitated for a moment. 'How shall I put it? No one has ever seemed...*quite right*. And although I have been, as you can imagine, under a considerable amount of pressure from my mother and various relatives to get married and settle down to producing the next generation to inherit the land and title, I've never been prepared to accept second best.

'To put it bluntly, my darling,' he told her firmly, 'I was simply not prepared to sacrifice my happiness—or anyone else's for that matter—by marrying somebody who might be regarded as "suitable", but with whom I was not truly in love.'

He fell silent for a moment, taking hold of her hand and absentmindedly running his thumb over the large emerald and diamond ring on her finger.

'And then, quite out of the blue, I caught sight of you at Mark and Sarah's wedding. Actually...' he gave a soft laugh '...I could hardly see anything of you—not at first. Just a brief, hurried impression, a fleeting glimpse of a tall slim girl, before she swiftly disappeared from sight. And even in the church—' he turned to frown at her '—you were making damned sure I hardly saw anything of you, right?'

She nodded. 'I was sick with fright,' she confessed. 'It all—I don't know. The past seemed to come up and hit me in the face, somehow,' she muttered, unable to fully express the sudden shock and consternation which she'd felt on meeting him again after such a long time.

'And you've grown,' he told her in a slightly aggrieved voice. 'You really *have* changed, Olivia. So it's no wonder I didn't recognise you straight away, is it? Then, when I discovered *who* you were...and after that first kiss, the night of the Rylands' wedding...I *knew*, without the shadow of any doubt, that you were the woman for me, and—well, you know the rest.'

'No—I don't!' she protested. 'You've been acting so peculiarly, and...'

'That's rich!' He grinned at her. 'Let me tell you that I've *never* been given such a hard time in all my life. Talk about a prickly pear! One moment you'd melt in my arms, and the next you were taking to your heels and sprinting away from me as fast as you could go! Quite frankly, I can't imagine any other man having a more exhausting courtship.'

'*Courtship?* What courtship?' She glared at him. 'And don't think that I haven't the gravest suspicions about your employment of Hugo,' she added accusingly.

'Ah, well…yes,' he murmured, a slightly sheepish expression flickering across his handsome face. 'I must admit that initially I was just digging away to try and find some lever—something I could possibly use to get closer to you, Olivia. Because, believe me, you've proved a very hard nut to crack.'

'Thanks!' she drawled grimly.

He laughed. 'You know what I mean. However, to return to the subject of Hugo, I have to say that I do think he's actually very talented indeed. As soon as I'd arranged—as anonymously as I could—to see the sort of work he was capable of producing, I immediately realised that I'd be incredibly foolish not to snap him up while the going was good.

'So, my darling,' he added, 'I can faithfully promise you that Hugo got the job solely on his own merits. And, really, you know, I may love you with all my heart but I'm not likely to jeopardise such a very important and highly expensive development simply for the sake of one of your lovely smiles.'

'I'm glad to hear it,' she murmured, suddenly feeling highly relieved to know that her brother had been quite right. In fact, it looked as though he deserved the success he was likely to achieve with his designs for the new village.

'However,' Dominic was saying, 'I do have to confess

the truth—which is that your brother didn't have to start work quite as soon as I insisted that he did. And, yes, I am guilty of quickly snapping up the subsequent vacancy in John Graham's chalet house party for my own nefarious ends! And now you know it all...' he murmured, leaning back on the red plush banquette, clearly highly relieved to have got rid of all the necessary explanations of his behaviour over the past weeks.

'Hmm...' Olivia muttered, before suddenly remembering another question which needed answering. 'Oh, yes— what on earth were you doing this morning, calling in to see my father?'

'Don't be ridiculous, darling—I had to ask his permission to marry you, didn't I?'

'Oh...right,' she murmured, realising that Hugo's joking comment had, after all, been quite correct. 'That's rather old-fashioned of you, isn't it?'

'Ah, but surely you must have realised by now that I'm a *very* old-fashioned man?' he told her with a low rumble of laughter, and was prevented from saying any more by the sharp ringing tone of his mobile phone.

'I'm sorry, I thought I'd switched the damn thing off,' he muttered irritably, removing the wafer-thin instrument from the pocket of his coat. Just about to cancel the call, he suddenly recognised the New York telephone number illuminated on the digital display.

'Hi, darling,' he murmured down the phone. 'I have to tell you that this is definitely *not* the right moment to phone me. Not when I've just placed an engagement ring on a girl's finger and— Oh, my God, Connie! How on earth did that happen?'

Olivia, who'd found herself stiffening when he'd begun the telephone conversation with someone who was clearly a close and intimate female friend, immediately relaxed as she realised that he must be talking to his sister, Connie, in the United States. A fact Dominic confirmed as, his lips tightening, his dark brows drawn together in a deep frown, he completed his call and sat staring down at the tablecloth for a moment, clearly buried in thought.

'Is there a problem?' she asked quietly.

He nodded. Yes...yes, I must catch the next flight to New York,' he told her, quickly beckoning to a waiter and requesting his bill.

'That guy my sister has been living with for some years—Lorne Vidal, the film and stage impresario—he's been involved in a bad traffic accident. According to Connie it's touch and go as to whether he's going to make it or not. So I must go to her.'

'Yes, of course you must,' she instantly agreed, rising from the table and, after being helped into her coat, accompanying him out of the restaurant.

'I'm so sorry about this, darling,' he told her as they walked the short distance up Holland Park Avenue between the restaurant and her own small house. 'I'll be back as soon as I can, of course. And in the meantime,' he added as he took the key from her hand and opened her front door, before gathering her into his arms for a swift, passionate kiss, 'just remember that I love you, hmm?'

And that was the last she'd seen of Dominic, Olivia told herself sadly, as she turned away from the depressing sight of grey clouds and wet, sodden lawns.

Sighing heavily, she forced herself to walk into the study, whose empty shelves provided mute testimony to the fact that the valuable leather-covered volumes which had once lined the walls had long since been sent to the London auction rooms. Another of her father's vain attempts to solve his various financial problems.

Poor Hugo. The only thing he was likely to inherit from their father was the title—which was virtually useless in this day and age. Because anything that could be sold had been got rid of long ago. And with the house itself heavily mortgaged, Olivia reckoned that there would be just enough left to pay her father's funeral expenses and, hopefully, a small lump sum for Mrs Douglas, in recognition of her kindness in looking after their old father.

Not much of a legacy for either herself or her brother, she told herself wryly, before realising that maybe she had been fortunate after all, since she had been impelled and forced to earn her own living. And maybe Hugo wouldn't have taken on his present profession if he'd had the soft cushion of wealth to fall back on. So, maybe they were lucky, after all.

Still not having heard from Dominic by the time the day of the funeral dawned, Olivia tried to find consolation in the thought that he would have had no idea or knowledge of her father's sudden death, or the fact that she'd been forced to leave Mo holding the fort in London while having to be at her old home in Kent, sorting out her father's affairs.

Standing beside Hugo in the front pew of the old village church, it seemed appropriate that the solemn words of the service should be accompanied by the steady rain falling down from the heavens. However, she would have given just about everything she possessed to have Dominic by her side when she spotted his mother amongst the mourners at the funeral service.

It was stupid of her not to have realised that the Dowager Countess of Tenterden was bound to attend the funeral of a close neighbour. And later, as she and her brother stood at the lych-gate following their father's burial in a far corner of the churchyard, shaking the mourners' hands and thanking those who'd clearly travelled a long way for the service, Olivia could feel herself becoming more and more nervous at the thought of coming face to face with Dominic's mother.

And, indeed, it really was a very awkward situation. Because, with Dominic having placed that announcement of their engagement in the papers over a week ago, his mother might reasonably expect to have been introduced to his new fiancée. Or, in her case, Olivia reminded herself quickly, to meet once again the woman whom she'd known as a young girl.

However, in the event—and probably thanks to the crowd of people standing about them—the encounter wasn't quite so frightening as she'd feared.

For one thing, the old Countess somehow seemed to have shrunk, and was no longer the tall, fearsome figure that Olivia remembered. In fact, it was distinctly unnerving to find herself staring *down* at the whip-thin, grey-haired old lady. Although she still bore an uncanny resemblance to her son, with the same arrogant nose and the similar grey all-seeing eyes beneath their heavy lids.

'Good morning, Olivia,' the Countess said briskly. 'I was sorry to hear about your father's death. In many ways he was a very good man. Although I don't think he would be too pleased to see *her*!' the old woman added, nodding to the other side of the road outside the church, where a large white Mercedes was drawn up at the verge. Leaning up against the bonnet, with a scarlet umbrella covering her coiffure in one hand and a long cigarette in the other, was a tall, thin blonde woman dressed in a highly inappropriate bright scarlet suit.

'Oh, my God!' Olivia gasped in horror.

'My sentiments exactly,' the Countess agreed with a

wintry smile. 'Dear Pamela never knew when *not* to make an entrance, did she?'

'You're so right!' Olivia hissed through gritted teeth, before being startled by the low rumble of laughter from the elderly woman standing beside her.

'Well, I must go, and leave you to the tender mercies of your ex-stepmother,' the Countess told her, pulling on her gloves. 'And although I won't say it wasn't a surprise—because it most certainly was—I'm looking forward to welcoming you into the family in the near future, Olivia,' she added with another one of her fleeting, icy smiles. 'You're not exactly what I had in mind for my son's bride. However, I'm now beginning to think that you might do very well—very well indeed.'

'Phew!' Hugo murmured as the old lady, with her back as straight as a ramrod, walked calmly away. 'I must say, Livvy, it sounds as though the old dragon does approve of you, after all!'

'That's the least of our worries,' she muttered out of the side of her mouth. 'Have you seen who's lounging against that car across the road?'

'Oh, Lord! That's all we need,' he groaned.

However, in the event, the totally unexpected appearance of her stepmother proved not to be the ordeal Hugo and Olivia had feared.

Possibly because Pamela had always possessed the hide of a rhinoceros, and was virtually unsnubbable, there was no doubt, as Hugo pointed out later, that when their stepmother had ordered her uniformed chauffeur to follow them back to their old family home, she had at least provided a diversion from having to return to an empty, unhappy house, containing just themselves and their memories.

'Hello, my darlings,' Pamela trilled as she marched

boldly into the house behind them. 'Yes, I know you don't want to see me,' she added with a shrill laugh, wrinkling her nose as she wandered through the virtually empty rooms whose contents had been sold long ago. 'However, believe it or not, I was sorry to hear about your father. Poor old boy—he never could come to terms with modern-day life, could he?'

There was just enough truth in that last statement to prevent Olivia from throwing the other woman out of the house, as she'd originally intended. Which didn't mean, of course, that she'd ever forgive her stepmother, either for ruining her father's life or, indeed, for making her own teenage years an utter misery. Still, her father was now dead, and she, herself, was a fully grown woman. And, as Dominic had firmly said to her, the past is history, and one should let it go and concentrate on living in the present.

'I thought you might be inviting some of the local squirearchy back for a drink after the funeral,' Pamela was saying. 'But of course I quite see that you couldn't do that—not with the house in this state. Incidentally,' she added peering about her, 'I don't suppose you've got a drink anywhere, have you?'

'No, I'm afraid we haven't,' Hugo told her firmly, almost as surprised as Olivia to find, with the passage of time, that he no longer felt such a sharp animosity towards his stepmother as he'd done in the past.

'Never mind,' Pamela told him with a smile, before going to the front door and ordering her chauffeur to bring in the large wicker hamper from the boot of the car.

'It's a bit of a drive down here from the north of England,' Pamela informed them, directing the chauffeur to take the hamper into the large kitchen. 'So I had my housekeeper put together a bit of a picnic, just in case I got hungry on the journey. And you two might not want a drink—but I could certainly do with one.'

This is totally bizarre! Olivia found herself thinking as she, Hugo and her stepmother sat around the kitchen table, munching Pamela's sandwiches and drinking coffee while Pamela tossed back two or three glasses of the cool white wine which she'd produced from the hamper.

'Well, I must say, Hugo, it's nice to see you looking so well,' Pamela told him. 'And *you've* done rather well for yourself, Olivia, I hear!' Pamela added with a laugh. 'But how on earth are you going to cope with that awful old trout of a mother-in-law? I should think that she's just about impossible to live with, don't you?'

'I really haven't thought about it,' Olivia murmured, despite knowing that she was telling an outright lie, and that Pamela, who was no fool, had accurately put her finger on a potentially difficult problem.

'Of course, I did you a great favour all those years ago,' her stepmother continued. 'I know you think I went completely off the deep end. But really, you were *far* too young. It wouldn't have lasted—his ghastly old mother would have seen to that, in any case. Far better to have nipped it in the bud, darling, and let that young man sow his wild oats before suddenly realising what he's been missing all these years,' she added sagely. 'And that's what happened, didn't it? So, you see, I really did you a favour after all, didn't I?'

'Yes, I suppose in a ghastly sort of way, you did,' Olivia agreed with a wry smile, as her stepmother stood up and said that it was time she left.

'God, what a day!' Hugo groaned, watching as the white Mercedes disappeared into the distance. 'It's strange, you know, but somehow I found that I didn't really hate old Pamela half as much as I thought I would.'

'No,' Olivia sighed. 'I had exactly the same thought. Still, I'd better get on with answering some more of those letters,' she said, before reminding him not to be late, tomorrow morning, for their appointment with the lawyer.

Exhausted by everything that had happened yesterday, it was some time before Olivia struggled up from the depths of a deep, heavy sleep the next morning, to hear a loud, determined banging of the knocker on the front door.

Rolling over to look at her bedside clock, she groaned as her sleep-laden eyes saw that it was only just seven o'clock.

It was *far* too early to be Hugo, who wasn't due to arrive until ten o'clock that morning. So maybe if she ignored the noise it would just go away.

It seemed as though she'd been right, as a deathly silence seemed to fall on the house. And she was just, once again, slipping back to sleep, when she heard a loud creak of the floorboard outside her room.

Oh, Lord. It *was* Hugo. What on earth had possessed him to arrive so early?

'Go away!' she moaned as she heard the door open and the sound of firm footsteps approaching the bed.

'Well! I don't call that much of a welcome. Not when I've just flown the Atlantic and driven straight down here from the airport,' a familiar voice grumbled loudly, before sitting down on the bed beside her. 'And as for your stupidity in not locking the back door—it's just as well that there's clearly nothing to steal in this house, or you'd have been a magnet for burglars!'

'*Dominic!*' she squeaked with joy, frantically wrestling with the bedclothes as she struggled to sit up. 'Oh, Dominic—I can't tell you how much I've missed you!'

she exclaimed, throwing her arms around his neck and bursting into tears.

'For heaven's sake!' she muttered some moments later, as he laughingly handed her a large white handkerchief to dry her tears.

'I'm really *not* the sort of person who's given to crying like this,' she assured him earnestly, gazing up into his handsome face, her dark eyelashes wet and spiky with tears. 'It's just…it's just that I've missed you so *very* much. My father died, and it's all been so awful, and…'

'I know, darling,' he murmured, lowering his head to kiss away the tears from her eyes, cradling her in his arms and rocking gently back and forth as if comforting a child.

Blissfully content within his embrace, she savoured the cold, fresh chill of his black cashmere overcoat against her soft cheek, and the cool touch of his hard, firm mouth as he lowered his head to savour the warmth of her trembling lips.

'Mmm…you're so deliciously warm and cuddly,' he murmured, before placing her against the pillows and standing up to remove his overcoat, swiftly followed by his dark formal suit, and silk tie.

'What on earth are you doing?' she mumbled, still half asleep and dazed with happiness at his return.

'I can tell you that it's damn cold outside. And your bed looks hugely inviting,' he said, clicking his teeth with irritation as one of his gold cuff-links obstinately refused to be undone. 'Besides,' he added, finally managing to remove his silk shirt, 'I'm starving!'

'Oh, no!' she groaned, snuggling back amongst the pillows. 'Have I *really* got to get up and cook you a meal?'

'Absolutely not!' he exclaimed with a rumble of laughter as he removed the rest of his clothing. 'When I said I was starving I was referring to the fact that I haven't made love to you for a whole week! In fact, I'll have you know that I'm a desperate man,' he announced dramatically, his mouth twitching with laughter as he gazed down at her.

'Yes.' She grinned back at him. 'I can definitely see *that*!' she murmured, desperately trying to control the eager anticipation of her own trembling body as she stared at his magnificently proportioned figure and the hard, firm evidence of his arousal. 'Well—hurry up and get into bed,' she laughed, throwing back the bedclothes. 'Believe me, Dominic, you're not the only one who's starving!'

'Oh, darling, this is so good!' he groaned, clasping her tightly in his arms, his kisses everything she'd hungered for during the past few deeply unhappy days.

'Oh, I forgot to ask…' she muttered as he removed her silk nightdress, his lips tracing its departure with lingering caresses. 'Your sister? Is the man she lives with all right? The car crash, I mean…' she added disjointedly, the touch of his mouth on her flesh making it difficult for her to concentrate on anything other than the man poised above her as he slowly caressed her trembling body.

'She's fine. He's recovering well. Now…for God's sake, Olivia—please shut up and let me make love to you!' he groaned.

And then there was no other reality save the soft, tender touch of his hands on her flesh, the pounding of her heart beating in rapid concert with his own, as she eagerly welcomed the powerful, thrusting passion and total possession of the man she loved with all her heart.

EPILOGUE

OLIVIA WAS ASTONISHED to find herself shivering with fright in the porch of the chapel at Charlbury Castle.

Surely after all her experience in arranging so many marriages...surely she ought to be the very *last* person to be suffering from stage fright—especially at her own wedding, for heaven's sake!

'Are you OK, Livvy?' Hugo asked, gazing anxiously down at the nervous, trembling figure of his sister.

Although why she should be so nervous he had absolutely no idea. Because, quite simply, he had never in all his life seen her looking quite so beautiful with her long tawny-gold hair flowing in a rippling stream down her back, held up at the crown of her head by a large antique diamond tiara—a family heirloom of the FitzCharles family—the only jewellery she was wearing other than a pair of large plain diamond studs in her ears and the magnificent diamond and emerald engagement ring, both of which had been presented to her by her future husband.

Olivia looked magnificent, he decided. Every inch a future countess. Her ultra-simple plain sheath dress, of finest pale ivory lace over thin silk of the same colour, shimmered down over her tall, slim figure, the long train in the same material flowing down from her waist at the back causing her to look remarkably sophisticated and elegant, with a delicate bouquet of small ivory roses and trailing green ivy completing the picture.

'I'm so relieved that you didn't have a whole tribe of little bridesmaids,' Hugo muttered thankfully. 'The last wedding I went to one of them was sick all over my shoes!' he added with a shudder.

'No, well, I would have liked some, but the decision sort of took itself,' she told him, trying to control her nervously chattering teeth. 'Not having any small children in the family, there seemed no point somehow.'

'You look wonderful!' Mo breathed from behind Olivia, where she was kneeling on the floor making the final adjustments to the train.

'For heaven's sake, Mo, don't worry about that,' Olivia muttered, turning to grin down at her assistant. 'Hurry up and go on into the church. There's no need to worry about me.'

But Mo, who'd absolutely insisted on organising every small detail of the wedding, merely shook her head as she rose to her feet.

'Oh, no! I'm going to see you safely down the aisle before I move from here,' she told her with a grin. '*I'm* in charge of this wedding—and don't you forget it!'

Smiling happily at her employee and good friend, Olivia couldn't help thinking how lucky she was. Not only in being just about to marry the man of her dreams, but also in having so many good friends. And most of them were already in the chapel, here at Charlbury Castle, to witness her marriage to Dominic before joining them at a reception in the castle to celebrate their marriage.

'I wish Dad was here,' she murmured to her brother, who nodded, both of them looking sad for a moment.

'Never mind, Livvy,' Hugo told her softly. 'I'll bet he's looking down from some cloud up there—and I know he'll be as pleased as punch that you're marrying Dominic. Mrs Douglas told me that he was absolutely thrilled to bits about your engagement. So stop worrying, OK?'

She nodded. This wasn't a day for sadness or regrets. It was a day to look forward. And indeed, when she thought about her future life, all her past fears and hesitancies seemed somehow totally unimportant.

Even the problem of how she was going to deal with her future mother-in-law seemed to have been solved to everyone's satisfaction. Because, quite astonishingly, it seemed that Augusta, Dowager Countess of Tenterden had finally decided that Olivia really *was* the perfect bride for her son.

'And to be utterly frank, my dear,' the old lady had told her, 'I reckon I've done my bit as far as the castle itself is concerned. Believe me, it's not much fun having the general public traipsing through one's sitting room most days in the summer. And since dear Dominic has arranged for the old tenants to leave the Dower House— and I've always wanted to get my hands on *that* particular garden!—I'm going to be only too happy to hand over the reins to you.

'Although,' she'd added reflectively, 'if I were you I'd be tempted to change the rooms around, and take one of the wings of the castle for your own private use. Much nicer—and, I need hardly say, much warmer in the winter. Heating that huge old hall is no joke! I often think half the reason I'm so thin is because I've shivered off any fat I might have had!' she'd added, with what, for the old lady, had clearly been a friendly smile.

And so, after checking with Dominic that his mother really *did* want to move from the castle, Olivia had realised that the last problem she'd faced over her marriage had been smoothly and easily removed.

Her thoughts were interrupted as Mo tapped her on the shoulder, nodding to where an usher was signalling that the wedding was about to begin.

'OK—here we go!' Hugo murmured as the organist began playing the first strong chords of the 'Trumpet Voluntary'.

She'd never...simply *never* felt so frightened in all her life, Olivia thought as she found herself walking slowly up the red carpet towards the tall, commanding figure of Dominic, with his best man, John Graham, standing beside him.

'Who else should I choose?' Dominic had laughed when she'd asked who he was intending to select as his best man. 'It has to be John—because without his invitation to join the chalet party you and I might never have got together, right?'

But now, with the organ music filling the ancient chapel, Olivia found herself suddenly panicking as to whether she was, in fact, going to be able to place one leg in front of the other on her progress up the long, long aisle.

And then, as Dominic slowly turned round to view the approach of his bride—and suddenly realised that his normally cool, calm and serene Olivia was almost paralytic with nervous tension—he instinctively came to her rescue.

Swiftly moving down the aisle towards her, and giving Hugo a brief smile of apology as he removed Olivia's hand from her brother's arm, he lowered his dark head to press a gentle kiss on her trembling lips.

'Just remember: I love you with all my heart,' he whispered softly, before firmly tucking her arm in his and leading her towards the altar and the start of their married life together—at last.

HARLEQUIN PRESENTS®

*invites you to see
how the other half marry in:*

SOCIETY WEDDINGS

This sensational new five-book miniseries invites
you to be our VIP guest at some of the most talked-
about weddings of the decade—spectacular events
where the cream of society gather to celebrate the
marriages of dazzling brides and grooms in
breathtaking, international locations.

Be there to toast each of the happy couples:

Aug. 1999—**The Wedding-Night Affair**, #2044,
Miranda Lee

Sept. 1999—**The Impatient Groom**, #2054,
Sara Wood

Oct. 1999—**The Mistress Bride**, #2056,
Michelle Reid

Nov. 1999—**The Society Groom**, #2066,
Mary Lyons

Dec. 1999—**A Convenient Bridegroom**, #2067,
Helen Bianchin

Available wherever Harlequin books are sold.

HARLEQUIN®
Makes any time special™

Coming Next Month

HARLEQUIN PRESENTS®

THE BEST HAS JUST GOTTEN BETTER!

#2067 A CONVENIENT BRIDEGROOM Helen Bianchin
(Society Weddings)
In her marriage of convenience to Carlo Santangelo, Aysha
knew she'd gain wealth, status and the sexiest husband ever!
Aysha loved her fiancé and wanted a real marriage, but would
Carlo give up his glamorous mistress...?

#2068 LOVER BY DECEPTION Penny Jordan
(Sweet Revenge/Seduction)
When Anna Trewayne lost her memory, she mistakenly
believed Ward Hunter to be a friend and lover. She'd
welcomed him into her arms...her bed...but what would
happen when her memory returned?

#2069 A MARRIAGE BETRAYED Emma Darcy
Kristy longed to find her natural family, but instead she found
Armand Dutournier, who wanted revenge for a betrayal she
hadn't committed. Did that mean she had a twin? Was he the
only lead to the family she yearned for?

#2070 THE YULETIDE CHILD Charlotte Lamb
(Expecting!)
Dylan had been thrilled when she'd married handsome
Ross Jefferson after a whirlwind romance. But she'd also
moved out of town and become unexpectedly pregnant.
Worse—her husband seemed to be having an affair....

#2071 MISTLETOE MISTRESS Helen Brooks
Joanne refused to have an affair with her sexy, arrogant
boss, Hawk Mallen. But then he offered her a dream
promotion—with one catch: she was at his command day
and night. Could she resist such a tempting proposal?

#2072 THE FAITHFUL WIFE Diana Hamilton
Jake and Bella, once happily married, have been separated a
whole year. Now Jake and Bella are tricked into spending
Christmas together. Isolated, they discover the passion is
still there—but can they overcome their past?